LEGION BOOK THREE

AWAKENING

A.D. STARRLING
AUTHOR OF THE SEVENTEEN SERIES

COPYRIGHT

PROLOGUE

1857, ENGLAND

It was the scream that woke him. The boy bolted upright in the four-poster bed, the sheets crumpling to his waist. He blinked before looking dazedly around his bedroom, the remains of his nightmare fading to wisps of darkness in the night. Moonlight washed through the leaded windows of the Victorian mansion in bright beams, illuminating the empty chamber around him.

For one wild moment, the boy wondered if the sound had been part of the terrible dream he'd been having. The same dream he'd experienced every night for the past month. The one where monsters dwelled.

The scream came again. This time, it spoke of unspeakable pain and terror.

A whimper left the boy's lips when he recognized his mother's tortured voice.

There was no longer any doubt in his mind. This, whatever was transpiring on this cold winter's night, was no dream.

Another voice joined his mother's desperate cries.

The boy's eyes widened as his father's horrified yells echoed down the west wing hallway.

He scrambled out of bed and stood frozen for a moment, the cold floorboards beneath his feet sapping away what little warmth remained in his body. His gaze found the poker by the fireplace.

The dying embers in the hearth painted a macabre red glow across the metal.

The boy walked over on trembling legs and closed his hand around the handle, his pulse racing with fear. More voices reached him.

His sisters were sobbing and begging, their tones rising with every desperate word they uttered, their panic so thick it paralyzed him once more. They stopped abruptly, their pleas cut off by a grisly, fleshy sound.

Deathly silence fell upon the mansion. The boy waited, mouth dry and heart pounding so fast he feared it would leap from his chest.

The noise that came next caused his bladder to loosen. Warm wetness pooled between his legs as an inhuman shriek tore through his home.

It was the same sound he'd heard the monsters in his nightmares make.

A heavy footfall made the floor tremble. Something was coming down the hallway toward his room. Something big. Something that scratched the wood with every wicked step.

A vile stench tickled the boy's nostrils.

A shadow appeared across the gap beneath his bedroom door. The floorboards dipped slightly as the monster stopped outside.

The boy took a step back. A gasp whooshed out of him

as he slipped on his own urine and landed heavily on his backside.

A scraping noise danced across the outside of the door, the sound setting the boy's teeth on edge even as he scrambled desperately to his feet.

"*Fie, foh, and fum,*" the monster growled, "*I smell the blood of an Englishman.*"

Tears overflowed the boy's eyes and ran down his icy cheeks. He swallowed the sobs rising in his chest.

His family was dead. He knew this without question.

And the monster who had murdered them, the one from his darkest nightmares, the one now standing outside his room, was going to kill him too. Terror and despair swamped him, a heavy mantle that weighed his small body down. His shoulders sagged. His fingers loosened around the poker.

There was no point fighting his fate.

Thump.

The boy blinked, the monster temporarily forgotten. Before he could fathom the eerie throbbing he'd just sensed inside the very marrow of his soul, the bedroom door exploded inward in a cloud of deadly shards and splinters. A cry left him, unbidden.

The monster appeared through the falling debris, reeking of death and rotting flesh. It was over six feet tall, with a hulking physique, its hands and feet tipped by wicked, blood-soaked talons. Its eyes were black but for their yellow centers.

The boy registered the gore and gristle coating the monster's lower face and realized he was looking at what remained of his parents and sisters. Rage erupted inside of him then, so sudden and so fierce he almost gasped with the force of it.

Thump-thump.

There was no time to explore the heavy beat that was matching his own frantic heart or the uncanny warmth rising from the depths of his body. The boy widened his stance and gripped the poker in white-knuckled fists, the fury he was experiencing echoed by something inside him. Something that he knew instinctively was not of this world.

Gone was the crippling fear that had gripped him a moment past. In its place was deadly determination.

Thump-thump. Thump-thump.

Heat bloomed on the boy's right palm. Though he caught a faint glow between his fingers out the corner of his eye, he did not dare look away from the monster who had just stepped inside his room.

To do so would be to invite instant death.

The boy and the monster stared at one another for a frozen moment in time. In the monster's obsidian eyes, the boy detected surprise and a hint of interest. The monster smiled, its features twisting in a ghastly grimace of loathing and hunger. It rushed toward the boy, its movements so swift he almost missed its charge.

White light filled the room.

CHAPTER ONE

OTIS BOONE EYED THE MOUTH OF THE ALLEYWAY ACROSS the road nervously. A summer rainstorm plummeted from the Chicago night sky, the showers rendered more forceful by the winds blowing off Lake Michigan.

He cleared the misted breath from his spectacles, pulled the hood of his coat low over his head, and darted between the traffic swishing along the avenue.

The hems of his trousers were wet by the time he entered the alley. He checked the address on his phone before studying the neon sign on the building halfway down the shadowy passage. The cracked light bars flickered dully, the bottom one intermittently cutting out. Otis swallowed.

This is the right place.

Trepidation churned his stomach. His instincts were yelling at him to turn around and walk out of there. His feet started to move almost unconsciously.

He stopped and fisted his hands.

There was too much at stake for him to turn tail now.

Otis clenched his jaw, marched up the alley, and strode inside the bar with more confidence than he felt.

The interior was just as murky as he'd expected it to be. It was also busy for a Tuesday night.

He made his way to the counter, ordered a beer, and headed into the back room. The reserved booth was at the far end, just as the man he was meeting had promised it would be. Otis took a seat with his back to the wall and huddled over his drink while he watched the crowd.

Artemus will kill me if he finds out about this.

His boss's default irate expression rose before his eyes, along with the faces of his new housemates. People Otis had met for the first time three months ago, on the day he discovered that the world he lived in was full of strange and fearsome creatures and that he was part of that extraordinary circle by virtue of his birth.

His mother's death was something that still weighed heavily on Otis's conscience. It was during her pregnancy that Catherine Boone had started to exhibit symptoms that would eventually lead to her confinement to a psychiatric hospital, the day after she gave birth to him. Even though there was no logical reason to blame himself, Otis had never been able to rid himself of the guilt that had plagued him ever since the day he discovered the details of what had led to her incarceration.

That her delusions and the journals she would go on to write over the years that followed were foreshadowings of events currently unfolding around the world at large had come as a shock to Otis. In contrast, his father William had seemed almost relieved to have his dead wife finally vindicated.

It was because of his mother's journals that Otis found himself in his present predicament. When Artemus had returned from L.A. with Haruki Kuroda, AKA the Colchian Dragon, in tow, he'd walked in on Otis trying to translate his mother's writings. He'd also discovered that the uncanny powers Otis had exhibited for the first time in the secret bunker where his father had been hiding under their family farm had grown stronger. It was with some reluctance that Otis had admitted to the strange dreams he'd started to have too. Dreams that hinted at his true origins.

The discovery of the names of the fathers of Artemus and his twin brother Drake had stunned Otis to the core, as had the identity of the demon commander they had defeated in L.A. In the weeks that followed, he'd started searching for someone, anyone who could help him decipher his mother's writings. For it had become clear to him that the events Artemus and his companions had found themselves at the center of were but the start of more ominous things to come.

The only clues they possessed to help prevent the upcoming Apocalypse foretold by Otis's mother were in her journals. Unfortunately, as Otis and his father before him had discovered, Catherine Boone had written a code within a code. One that even the Vatican had been unable to decrypt.

It was desperation that had led Otis to the dark web four weeks past. And it was in one of the chat rooms there that he'd eventually stumbled across someone who had come up with a plausible lead.

A shadow fell across Otis. He looked up at the hulking figure who'd stopped next to his table and did his best to mask the gut-wrenching fear suddenly twisting through him.

"Dark Lord?" the giant mumbled.

Otis swallowed. He'd come up with the alias on the spur of the moment and now regretted it. "Wasp?"

The giant nodded and took the seat opposite him. "I can't stay for long. I have the nightshift at work."

Relief flooded Otis. The guy wasn't anywhere as menacing as he'd first come across. "Thanks for arranging this meeting."

The giant dipped his chin shyly. "To be honest, I was kinda curious about you. Although you're mostly quiet in the chat rooms, whenever you do speak up, it's always interesting. That's why I thought of you when I heard this story."

Otis's pulse accelerated. "What is it about?"

The giant looked around the bar to make sure no one else was within earshot, leaned toward Otis, and started to talk in a low voice.

Otis's eyes slowly widened as he listened.

CHAPTER TWO

ARTEMUS ADJUSTED THE KNOT IN HIS TIE, SHRUGGED into his suit jacket, and opened the top drawer of his dresser. He removed a small leather box from under a pile of personal items and lifted the lid. An old, automatic watch sat in a slot in the black, velvet lining inside.

A bout of melancholy washed through him as he turned the watch over and ran a finger across the inscription on the back. He sighed, fastened it around his wrist, and left the bedroom. A maze of corridors led him to the mansion's main staircase. He followed the smell of coffee to the kitchen.

Serena was reading a newspaper at the table that dominated the cozy, sunlit room. Artemus was about to ask her why she insisted on having the publication delivered to the mansion when she could just as easily peruse it online when a clatter of keys distracted him.

"And that, my furry little friend, is how you make some dough," Haruki muttered where he sat cross-legged on the window seat, a laptop on one knee and a chocolate Rex rabbit in his lap. He looked up at Artemus. "Oh. Hi, Art."

Artemus frowned at his newest tenant. "I told you not to call me that." He indicated the rabbit staring raptly at the computer screen. "Please tell me you're not doing something stupid like teaching him how to gamble."

Haruki grinned and removed the lollipop hanging from the corner of his mouth. "Nope. Just showing this little guy some basic business skills." He scratched the rabbit's head. "I gotta say, he's a natural at this."

Smokey the hellhound huffed, his eyes shrinking into slits of contentment at Haruki's petting.

Artemus grabbed a cup from a cabinet. "A natural at what? The only thing he seems to be good at is eating a hole in my life savings."

Serena turned over a page. "The rabbit just made a hundred grand on the London stock exchange."

Artemus nearly dropped the cup. "*What?!*"

Haruki's grin widened. "Like I said, he's a natural. His bank account is looking pretty healthy. Once he hits seven figures, they'll assign him a fund manager."

Artemus stared from Haruki to Smokey before stabbing an accusing finger at the rabbit. "He has a *bank account?!*"

Serena licked a finger and turned another page. "Callie opened one for him last month." The super soldier looked up from the article she was reading and gave Artemus a withering look. "You know, you should really keep up with this stuff, considering you're his owner."

A low growl erupted from Smokey's throat. He glared at Serena, his gaze alight with a hellish red glow.

Serena grimaced. "Alright, I take it back. Goldilocks is not your owner."

Smokey stopped growling. He let out a disgruntled sniff and switched his attention back to Haruki's laptop.

Artemus rolled his eyes. He wasn't even going to begin to question how Callie had gotten a bank account for the rabbit. "Well, if that's the case, he can start buying his own Kobe beef. And his litter."

Serena arched an eyebrow. "I thought he did his business outside."

"He usually does. Except someone keeps sneaking him bottles of expensive sake." Artemus glowered at Haruki. "Turns out a drunk hellhound has about as much control over his bladder as a human."

"Our beasts are bonding," Haruki said, unrepentant.

"Your beast is a drunkard," Artemus retorted. "At least the sake neutralizes his pee. Otherwise he would have burned a hole straight through the house and all the way to China by now." He turned to Serena and cocked his chin at her steaming coffee mug. "What's today's special?"

"Roasted Arabica with hazelnut and vanilla."

Artemus stuck his cup under the sleek chrome and silver monstrosity taking pride of place on the counter and pressed a button. An electronic buzz sounded from the device.

It was Nate's new toy and the latest in a range of coffee machines the super soldier was trying out. He'd even gotten into the habit of roasting and grinding his own beans every night and was in the middle of experimenting with flavors.

"Anyone seen Drake?"

"He went into town to get some supplies," Haruki said.

The fragrant aroma of Nate's latest concoction filled the kitchen.

Artemus lifted the cup to his lips. "And Nate?"

"Out for a run," Serena murmured.

Artemus raised his eyebrows. "I thought your

nanorobots and weird-ass super soldier DNA kept you guys fit."

"That's gold from someone who turns into a giant, flying pigeon," Serena said coolly. "Nate just has something on his mind. Running helps."

Artemus pondered this while he took a sip of the rich drink. He let out a sigh of satisfaction. "God, Nate is the best."

He became aware of a battery of stares.

"You're dressed nice," Serena said.

Smokey wrinkled his nose curiously at Artemus.

"Yeah, dude, what's with the suit?" Haruki's puzzled expression suddenly cleared. "Wait. Have you got a date?" He sucked in air. "Is it the infamous chick with the blue eyes? The one you keep having sex dreams about?"

Artemus gave the Yakuza heir a dirty look.

"That's pretty blasé of you, considering you're his bride and all," Serena told Haruki.

Haruki's amused smile faded to a scowl. "I am *not* his bride!"

"Your father would disagree. As would most of your henchmen. I swear Ogawa is contemplating writing some gay fan fic based on your coupling."

Artemus finished his coffee and left them bickering in the kitchen. He stepped out the back door, headed down the porch steps, and strolled toward the private cemetery that occupied a third of the eight-acre estate that surrounded his home.

Artemus lifted his face to the sky. A faint haze filled the heavens, filtering the rays of the sun to a golden glow. Yesterday's rainstorm had cleared. It was a bright summer morning and the perfect day for a memorial service.

Shadows engulfed him as he exited the burial grounds

of the LeBlanc family and entered the woodland that shielded the estate from the outside world. The mausoleum appeared between the trees a moment later, its pale marble walls gleaming in the sunlight.

The bronze doors were open. A man stood waiting on the threshold, his burly figure clad in a dark blue suit.

A twig cracked behind Artemus. He glanced over his shoulder and spied Smokey catching up to him. The rabbit met his gaze, his expression sheepish.

"Alright, you can tag along. But no peeing inside the crypt."

They stepped out from the treeline into the clearing that wrapped around the building.

"Hi," Elton LeBlanc murmured.

Artemus dipped his chin at his oldest friend and mentor. "Hey."

Elton studied Smokey with a faint frown but didn't say a word. They headed inside the mausoleum.

Yellow light flickered across the interior of the octagonal chamber from the candles glowing on the windowsills and the altar. Rising in the middle of the floor on a pedestal was a marble sarcophagus. A wreath had been laid upon it and fresh flowers sat in a vase at the base.

Artemus stared at the hamper and blanket next to it. "You brought a picnic?"

Elton shrugged. "It's a nice day. I thought he'd appreciate it."

He removed a slim bible from his jacket and opened it. Artemus took a deep breath and swallowed past the sudden lump in his throat as Elton started reciting a prayer.

Today marked the sixth anniversary of Karl LeBlanc's

death, Elton's older brother and the man Artemus had long considered his father.

Much had happened in the time since Elton had discovered Karl dying of what Artemus had presumed to be a heart attack in the alley behind the antique shop that had been in their family for generations.

For one thing, Artemus had only recently found out that Karl had not in fact died of natural causes like he had originally been told, but had been murdered by demons.

The same demons Elton had started investigating after his brother's death, his zealous quest eventually leading him to Rome and the Vatican organization he would be invited to join in the beginnings of a war against the inhuman creatures that now dwelled amongst mankind.

The same demons who had broken into Elton's auction house three months ago and attempted to steal an artifact that belonged to Callie Stone, the widow of one of the richest men in the country and the human chosen by the Chimera to be her host.

The same demons that Artemus and his newfound allies had battled most recently in L.A., where they had met Haruki Kuroda, the Yakuza heir whose soul was the vessel for the Colchian dragon.

The demons who belonged to a group known only as Ba'al.

CHAPTER THREE

"Any news on the Vatican mole?" Artemus asked Elton as they walked back to the house an hour later.

Elton shook his head. "No. Whoever it is, they're likely keeping a low profile. I would too if I had Vatican investigators looking for me."

Artemus frowned. It had been two months since their return from L.A. and the battle that had cost the life of Daniel Delacourt, the demon commander and leader of the L.A. branch of Ba'al. What Delacourt had revealed to them on the night they defeated him still weighed heavily on Artemus's mind. Not only had the man told them the identity of the demon prince who dwelled inside him, he had also disclosed the name of Artemus's father and that of the demon who had sired Drake, Artemus's twin brother.

"What about Ba'al?"

"No news on them either," Elton said, his tone troubled. "The Vatican hasn't sent us any information on their recent activities. Which is worrying in itself."

Artemus had to concur. Though Ba'al had suffered a

crushing blow after their battles in New York and L.A., they were too powerful an organization to simply retreat into the shadows and lick their wounds. They were up to something. He was certain of it.

They reached the house and walked around to the front porch and Elton's town car. A tall, thickset black man stepped out of the vehicle.

"Hi, Shamus," Artemus murmured.

Shamus Carmichael nodded a greeting. "Hey, Artemus."

A retired boxer and three-time world heavyweight boxing champion, Shamus was the head of Elton's security team at his auction house. He was also a member of the Vatican organization Elton belonged to and had fought alongside Artemus and his new allies against Ba'al.

"I'm having a small gathering at my place next Saturday." Elton climbed into the back seat of the town car. "Why don't you and the others come along? I'll send you an invite."

Artemus raised an eyebrow. "Is the widow gonna be there?"

Elton's expression grew stiff. "Yes, Helen will be there."

Artemus bit back a grin. Elton had started dating a retired university professor who lived down the road from him, much to the amusement of Artemus and Elton's team. It was difficult to picture the dignified Elton LeBlanc flirting with anyone.

He sobered when he recalled what they'd just been talking about.

"Do you think there are other gates to Hell?" Artemus asked Elton quietly as Shamus switched on the ignition. "Ones we don't know about yet?"

"I would bet money on it," Elton replied grimly. "Keep your guard up. Ba'al is bound to be looking for all of you."

Artemus watched the vehicle head down the drive, a thoughtful frown on his face. As frustrating as it was, there wasn't much he and the others could do right now.

It's not as if we can just find these gates on our own. They could be anywhere in the world. His frown deepened. *But if there are other gates, that means there are other Guardians too.*

Artemus sighed. Worrying about it wasn't going to achieve anything. He looked down at Smokey.

"Wanna come to the shop with me?"

The rabbit huffed his assent.

"Let me change out of this suit."

Artemus was about to head inside the house when the rumble of a powerful engine reached his ears. A black BMW superbike was coming up the mansion's driveway. It raised a small cloud of dirt as it pulled up next to them.

The rider removed his helmet and ran a hand through his dark tousled hair.

"Hey, Fuzzface," Drake murmured to Smokey. His gaze shifted to Artemus. "Look who I bumped into outside the estate."

He cocked a thumb at the man clinging to the back of the bike as if his life depended on it.

Artemus stared at his assistant. "What's up? I was just about to head down to the shop."

"We need to go to Salem," Otis Boone stated adamantly, his face pale. "I think I may have found someone who can decipher my mother's journals."

～

"HOW DID YOU FIND THIS GUY AGAIN?" SERENA SAID.

"I joined a group on the dark net two weeks ago," Otis replied awkwardly. "They specialize in all things esoteric. One of the guys I'd been chatting with messaged me last night. We met at a bar in Chinatown and he told me a rumor he'd just heard. About a mysterious man in Salem who owns an arcane bookstore. He's apparently a collector of rare books and is incredibly well versed in ancient languages." He paused. "According to the guy I met, this man is an urban legend in the collectible books world. There are all sorts of wild stories circulating about him."

Haruki made a face. "Those dark net people can be a bit far out when it comes to their conspiracy theories. You sure this guy and his bookstore even exist?"

"I have an address," Otis said tentatively.

Drake studied Artemus's assistant where he perched nervously on a chair at the kitchen table.

Several months had passed since they'd discovered that the young man Artemus had hired to work for him two years ago was in fact one of them. As in, he was a human who possessed supernatural abilities similar to the powers that resided inside Artemus, Drake, Callie, Haruki, and Smokey. Abilities that had awakened while he was still inside his mother's womb, on the very night that Artemus and Drake's lives had changed forever, when their own powers had manifested themselves for the first time.

Drake frowned faintly. *Although, we still don't know* what *Otis is.*

It was Otis's mother's journals that had helped them uncover Ba'al's identity after their first battle with the demonic organization in New York. Written while in the grip of the visions her unborn child was projecting to her, Catherine Boone had spent the latter third of her pregnancy and the sixteen years that followed penning a collection of journals and drawings that heralded an upcoming Apocalypse. Not the Apocalypse depicted in the bible, but a second, earlier Judgement Day. One that Hell wanted to bring to Earth. The same Judgement Day Daniel Delacourt, the demon commander they'd defeated in L.A., had spoken of.

"And you think this guy can decode your mother's writings?" Artemus said.

Drake could hear the skepticism in his twin's voice. Considering the Vatican hadn't been able to translate Catherine Boone's journals with all the experts at their disposal, the chances of some random bookstore owner in Salem being able to do so seemed farfetched.

Still, they needed the answers that were in those notebooks. Because what had become clear in L.A. was that Ba'al knew more about them and their powers than they did themselves. Drake suspected they also knew the identity of the demon inside him.

"It's the only lead I've found so far." Otis took his glasses off and pinched the bridge of his nose. "And the nightmares are getting worse."

Shortly after their return from L.A., Otis had admitted that he'd been having strange dreams ever since they'd paid a visit to his father in Pittsburg. From what he'd been able to deduce, his nightmares were also visions, not just of the future but the past too.

"You seen anything that looked like they could be gates to Hell in your dreams?" Artemus asked.

Serena stared at Artemus. "You think there are more of them?"

"Yes," Drake's twin replied, his expression perturbed.

Otis shook his head. "I'm not sure. They're always so," he waved a hand vaguely, "—fragmented." He looked at them anxiously. "I've started seeing these people. Strangers I've never met before. Men and women who appear to possess unique abilities too. But their powers are different from ours. They are strong. Very strong. In fact," he hesitated, "—I get the feeling they can survive death itself."

Serena straightened in her seat before exchanging a guarded glance with Nate. Unease filtered through Drake.

"Those people sound like Immortals," Artemus said, his eyes darkening with the same disquiet running through Drake.

Otis blinked in surprise. They'd told him about the Immortal race Isabelle Mueller and Mark Daniels, two of Elton's security people, belonged to. It was Mark's death and subsequent revival during their first encounter with Ba'al that had blown the cover of the two Immortal agents who had infiltrated Elton's security team.

According to Isabelle, the existence of the Immortal race was a closely guarded secret known to only the highest members of the Vatican hierarchy and a handful of world leaders. Although Serena and Nate seemed to have insider knowledge of them, they had always refused to discuss the matter, citing a promise all super soldiers had made to the Immortal society that had rescued them from certain death when they were but children.

"You're right," Otis mumbled. "They could very well be Immortals."

"What about the places you saw these people in?" Haruki asked curiously. "Anything there that might give us an idea as to where they could be?"

Otis stared at his hands. "The setting is always some kind of battle. And I think—I think they all took place in the past. One of them seemed to be from several thousand years ago even." He looked up at Artemus, his expression uneasy. "There's this one dream I had a week ago. It was different from the others. I had it again last night. All those strangers from my recent visions? They were together. And there was a woman with them. One with chocolate-colored hair and blue eyes."

Drake saw his twin stiffen.

"Are you sure?" Artemus said tensely.

Otis dipped his chin. "I think she might be the one you asked me about before. The girl from your dreams."

It was following their return from L.A. that Artemus had told them about the recurrent dream he'd had since the night he turned six, when his powers first awakened. A dream of a girl who had been as young as he was at the time but who had grown with him over the years.

"So, when do we leave?" Haruki said.

Artemus narrowed his eyes. "For someone who's done nothing these past two months except play on his computer, you're remarkably eager all of a sudden."

Haruki frowned. "That 'playing', as you put it, made the Kuroda Group ten million this month."

Artemus stared. "Maybe I should raise the rent."

Serena scowled. "Hey, just because Callie and the Yakuza kid are loaded doesn't mean everyone else is."

"Yeah," Drake muttered.

Haruki bristled at the super soldier. "I told you to stop calling me that."

Serena raised her eyebrows. "Which bit, Yakuza or kid?"

"Callie won't be back from her business trip until tomorrow," Nate said while Serena and Haruki started squabbling. "I'll stay here until she gets home."

Though he'd just returned from a ten-mile run, the

super soldier was barely sweating as he stood in his running shorts and T-shirt.

"You sure?" Artemus said.

Nate nodded. "Yes. Besides, I have...something I need to talk to her about."

CHAPTER FOUR

Sebastian Theodore Dante Lancaster closed the boiler room door and engaged the deadbolts. He removed his gloves from the pockets of his trousers before slipping them on fastidiously. Though he loathed being without them for any length of time, he'd had no choice but to take the gloves off for this particular task.

He crossed the shadowy basement and stepped inside a chrome and gold birdcage elevator. The accordion door rattled as he pulled it closed behind him. He stared at the orange glow visible through the narrow glass window at the top of the boiler room door with a faint frown while the elevator started its ascent.

It was a while before he reached the first floor of his home. Sebastian stepped out into the rear hall of the building, waved a hand absentmindedly across the wall, and headed upstairs to his private quarters. He removed the roast pheasant and vegetables he'd put in the cooking range earlier that afternoon and dined by candlelight with a leftover bottle of French Pinot Noir.

It was nine by the time he retired to his study. He

poured himself a glass of port from a crystal decanter, slipped Bach's Concerto for Two Violins on the gramophone, and settled into a parlor chair with a sigh. This was his favorite time of day and he was determined to savor it, especially tonight. He picked up the book of poetry on the side table next to the chair and lost himself in the rhythm of the words penned in pretty, cursive script while music echoed around the room.

"You sure this is the right place?" Artemus asked skeptically.

"I think so," Otis replied, his tone uncertain. He looked at the piece of paper in his hand. "It should be at the end of this alley. Number 117."

Artemus studied the deserted passageway they'd entered with a frown.

It had been two hours since they'd landed at Boston's Logan International Airport and made their way to Salem in a rental car. The address Otis's dark net friend had given him had brought them to the center of the coastal town, some half a mile west of the harbor. Night had fallen by the time they ventured into the historic district bathed in the warm, orange glow of the Victorian gas lamps that lined its thoroughfares.

They walked past an art gallery and two coffee shops as they headed deeper into the alley. Shadows swallowed them when they negotiated a corner after some hundred feet. The sounds of the main street faded behind them. Another turn came up ahead. They took it and drew to a halt some thirty feet later.

A redbrick wall stood at the end of the passage.

"It's a dead end," Drake said.

"Sure looks like it," Serena muttered.

Haruki grimaced. "You mean we came all this way for nothing?"

Otis looked crestfallen.

"Maybe we should ask around," Artemus suggested to his assistant. "It could be the address that guy gave you was wrong."

Otis hesitated before dipping his chin. They twisted on their heels and started back the way they'd come. Artemus stopped a couple of seconds later. He cast a puzzled look over his shoulder.

"You coming?"

Smokey hadn't moved. He was sitting on his rump and was staring intently at the redbrick wall.

Artemus frowned. The others paused a short distance away before slowly returning to his side.

"What's wrong?" Serena said quietly.

"I don't know," Artemus muttered. "Something's caught his atten—"

He tensed. The rabbit had transformed into his midnight black, hellhound form.

Otis gasped. A wicked blade appeared in Serena's right hand. Drake whipped his knife out from inside his jacket. Haruki's juzu bracelet shifted into a flaming sword.

The wing marks on Artemus's back trembled as he too reached inside himself to the source of his ungodly powers, his senses on high alert.

Smokey glanced at them, his eyes flashing red for an instant.

Do not be alarmed. It is not demons that I sense.

With that, the hellhound stepped through the wall and disappeared from their sight.

Serena startled. "What the—?"

"Where—where did the rabbit go?!" Otis stammered in a shaky voice.

Artemus walked up to the wall, his heart pounding. He could feel something now. Something faint. Something that was resonating with the unearthly energy coursing through his veins.

Haruki stopped beside Artemus, his puzzled gaze locked on the place where Smokey had disappeared. "What is that?"

Artemus knew the Yakuza heir was detecting the same vague thread of power he was feeling. "I don't know."

He hesitated before placing a hand on the brick wall. It remained as solid as it looked.

Artemus's skin prickled. His eyes widened at what he could sense under his fingertips. He took a step back, removed his switchblade from his boot, and released the double-edged sword within it.

"What are you—?" Drake started.

Artemus ignored his brother, poured power into his blade, and stabbed it through the wall. White light bloomed around his sword as it started to sink into the bricks. The red blocks he'd cut through trembled and shimmered, as if caught in a breeze. He clenched his jaw and moved the blade until he'd carved the outline of an opening large enough for them to pass through.

"Artemus?" Otis mumbled.

"What the hell did you just do?" Serena asked in a hard voice.

Artemus studied the glimmering doorway. "I think this is some kind of barrier."

He took a step toward it.

"Hey, wait a minute!" Haruki grabbed Artemus's arm.

"You know those stories where people walk through a glowing portal and end up somewhere totally different from their own world?"

"What, like Narnia?" Serena said.

"That was a wardrobe," Drake muttered.

"Yeah, what about it?" Artemus asked Haruki.

Haruki scowled. "Well, this could be one of those. We don't know what's on the other side."

"Tell you what, if we meet a giant talking lion, I'm sure your dragon will be more than a match for it. Besides, I'm pretty confident whoever made this barrier is someone we want to talk to."

Artemus ignored their troubled expressions and headed through the doorway. There was a brief feeling of resistance and warmth. Then he was through and out the other side. Cool night air brushed across his skin, bringing with it the smell of the nearby sea.

Smokey was sitting some thirty feet ahead of him.

Artemus joined the hellhound and gazed at the three-story building looming before them. It was dark but for the glow of the sign above the imposing, wooden front door.

Footsteps sounded behind them.

Artemus looked over his shoulder and was unsurprised to see the portal closing behind Drake, Serena, Haruki, and Otis.

"Well, I'll be damned," Serena muttered.

"This is the place," Otis gushed, his apprehension replaced by excitement. "'The Illuminated Scroll.'"

They stared at the bookstore.

CHAPTER FIVE

SEBASTIAN OPENED HIS EYES. HE GAZED DROWSILY AT the book on his lap and realized he'd fallen asleep. He shifted in the armchair, removed his watch from the breast pocket of his vest, and glanced at the time. The hour was indeed late. He swallowed a yawn behind one hand and was about to place the tome of poetry on the side table when he stiffened.

He had just registered two crucial details.

The first was a disruption in the protective barrier that he had painstakingly erected around his home. The second was the faint noise that had just travelled through the ornate metal vent next to the fireplace at the head of the study.

Sebastian frowned. There was no doubt about it.

Some pests had broken into his house.

He rose, walked over to the vent, and knelt to press his ear against the grille. Voices echoed up toward him.

~

"WHOSE PLAN WAS THIS AGAIN?" SERENA SAID morosely. "Oh yeah. The guy who always comes up with the bright ideas."

"Shut up," Artemus muttered.

"It *is* rather cramped," Otis mumbled.

"What I want to know is who gave the hellhound beans for lunch," Drake grumbled. "It smells like a dead man's ass in here."

"Sorry," Haruki murmured.

Smokey looked over his shoulder and twitched his nose at them, expression abashed. He hopped on ahead in his rabbit form, his hellhound one too big to fit in the ventilation duct.

Artemus sighed and carried on crawling through the copper pipe.

He'd spotted a hint of steam coming out of a grate near the base of the building when they'd been walking around it trying to figure out how to get inside. There were no windows that they could see and Drake had been unable to crack the ornate lock on the front door. It had even resisted a kick from Serena. Artemus had tried manipulating the metal in a last-ditch attempt to break in, only to discover yet another mysterious barrier protecting the lock.

He'd assumed the conduit would lead them to the bookstore's basement. Ten minutes in and there seemed to be no end to the damn thing. If anything, they were headed deeper underground, having already negotiated several shallow drops.

"Is it me or is it getting warmer in here?" Artemus murmured after a while, beads of perspiration forming on his forehead.

"It's not just you," Drake grunted.

Artemus looked over his shoulder and saw he wasn't the only one sweating. Something flared faintly at the other end of the pipe.

Artemus froze. "Oh shit."

Serena stopped where she was crawling on all fours at the back of their line. "What?" She followed Artemus's gaze and tensed. "The hell?!"

Artemus turned to Smokey. "You need to do the biggest pee you can, *right now!*"

Smokey's widening eyes reflected the expanding ball of pure, hot white light hurtling along the pipe toward them.

Drake cursed before twisting around and scrambling past Serena. The watch on his wrist glinted and transformed into a metal shield. It clunked against the sides of the duct, its shape incomplete.

"That thing will burn you!" Serena snarled.

"You forget," Drake said grimly. "I have a demon living inside me."

"Last time I checked, that didn't stop you from getting hurt!"

Haruki clambered past Otis and Serena, the skin on his hands and face glittering as he prepared to transform. "My scales can probably resist the heat!"

"Don't!" Artemus barked. "If you shapeshift in here, you'll crush—"

The rest of his words whooshed out of him as the pipe gave way in a cloud of acid vapor. They fell out of the hole Smokey had made in the ventilation duct, fire gushing through the jagged opening in their wake and licking their boots briefly.

Artemus caught a glimpse of an immense space spanning several stories as they plummeted helplessly through the air. It was surrounded on all sides by what looked to be galleries full of bookcases behind ornate, cast-iron balconies. His stomach twisted when he spied the distant, checkered floor at the bottom of the atrium.

Artemus saw Smokey falling next to him and reached out blindly. His fingers closed on soft, warm fur. Smokey huffed a sound of relief as Artemus hugged him to his chest.

"We need our wings!" Drake shouted somewhere above him.

Artemus sensed his twin's powers spike as he prepared to transform. He clenched his teeth. They had no choice but to shapeshift into their full forms if they wanted to survive the fall and save the others. Heat bloomed inside him as his own energy erupted. The wing marks on his back fluttered.

Someone grabbed his left wrist.

Artemus gasped as he came to an abrupt halt mid-air, the tendons in his arm screaming. Smokey scrabbled frantically at his shirt with his claws. Artemus steadied the rabbit's weight with one hand and looked up, his heart thumping.

Haruki was clutching him grimly.

Drake was holding onto the Yakuza heir. Above them, Serena grasped Drake's forearm with one hand and the edge of a giant, glittering, crystal chandelier with the other.

"Hang on," the super soldier said between gritted teeth.

She shifted her weight and started to swing them toward the closest balcony.

Artemus looked around wildly. "Where's Otis?!"

"I'm here," someone mumbled tremulously above Serena.

Relief flooded Artemus when he saw his assistant's face appear from where he'd been hugging the top of the chandelier.

"You're gonna have to jump at the same time we do!" Serena told Otis.

What little color remained in Otis's face disappeared. "I don't think I can."

"You have to!" Artemus said.

His stomach lurched as the arc of their swing got wider and wider, the chains securing the chandelier to the distant roof groaning ominously above them.

"Get ready," Serena warned. "*Now!*"

She let go at the peak of their next swing. They sailed over the edge of the closest balcony with mere inches to spare and landed hard on a wooden floor.

Artemus rolled and collided heavily with a bookcase, his arms wrapped protectively around Smokey. Blood pounded in his ears when he finally lurched to a rest on his back. He rose on one elbow and rubbed the back of his head with a wince.

"Ow."

Smokey wriggled out of his grasp and hopped over to the balcony. He shifted into his dark hellhound form, leapt atop the railing, and snatched the sleeve of Otis's jacket just as Artemus's assistant started to fall from where he'd been clinging desperately to a metal spindle. The hellhound jumped back onto the gallery floor, Otis thudding beside him with a groan.

A loud creak erupted behind Artemus. He looked over his shoulder. His eyes widened. He sat up and backpedaled hastily toward the others as the bookcase he'd struck tilted precariously. It landed heavily against the next one. The latter started to fall.

"That's not good," Haruki said dully.

They climbed to their feet and stared as the bookcases slowly toppled one after the other around the entire length and width of the gallery, their precious contents scattering to the floor while wood smashed thunderously against wood.

The last bookcase finally crashed into the first one. A couple of books bounced and rolled across the ground before striking Artemus's boots with a faintly accusatory thump.

"Wow," Serena said.

"Like a stack of dominos," Drake muttered.

They all looked at Artemus.

"Oh, come on!" he protested. "That could have happened to any one of—"

The air shivered with a violent burst of power. Artemus's ears popped.

"I was prepared to overlook your incursion upon my home, since you appear to possess some rather intriguing abilities," a voice growled in a deep and distinctively British accent. "But this? This—*horrible transgression?!* This I most certainly *cannot* forgive!"

A man stepped out from the shadows between a pair of bookcases to Artemus's left. He was dressed in beige striped pants, a white dress shirt with button cuffs, and a double-breasted tweed vest with a chain hanging out of the left pocket. A paisley cravat and polished dark boots completed his old-fashioned outfit.

There was a black leather glove on his left hand. His right hand was exposed. It currently contained a ball of pulsing, white light. The same light glowing from his eyes.

CHAPTER SIX

SEBASTIAN GLARED AT THE INTRUDERS WHO HAD invaded the library under his bookstore.

There were four men, a woman, and a large, fearsome black dog of indeterminate breed. He could sense subtle pulses of power coming from three of the men and the hound. The woman felt strange too, although he could not put a finger on what it was exactly that he was detecting from her. The fourth man with the glasses was as ordinary a human as he had ever come across.

The blond man who appeared to be their leader took a step toward him. "Look, we didn't mean to—"

Sebastian scowled and blasted them with the lightning ball in his right hand. The explosion filled the gallery with a burst of blinding brilliance. Books and torn pages fluttered around him as the thunderous boom started to die down, the waves from the detonation ruffling his carefully coiffed hair. He clenched his jaw.

It will take days to put these tomes back together. Those imbeciles!

The smoke finally cleared. Surprise darted through Sebastian.

The intruders were still standing, albeit in a half-crouch. A creature stood protectively before them, body glinting faintly as dying sparks of static electricity leapt across the silver scales covering his skin.

Sebastian realized it was one of the men. The Asian one.

Except he no longer looked human.

The creature's pupils were vertical slits aglow with a savage, orange light. The same light that was throbbing faintly under the scales covering his chest and belly, where Sebastian's blast had torn his shirt asunder. Wicked spikes protruded from his head and spine and the long, thick tail jutting from his tailbone. Pale horns framed his mandibles and the silver plates covering his cheeks and jawline. Smoke curled from his nostrils and the corners of his mouth.

In his right hand was a pale sword blazing with red flames.

The Dragon glowered at Sebastian. "I am officially pissed off."

The group huddling behind him slowly straightened. They were unharmed, the creature having taken the brunt of Sebastian's attack.

"Well, at least we know your scales can stop his—whatever the heck he just threw at us," the woman murmured with a scowl.

Sebastian ignored their exchange, his gaze riveted to the weapon in the beast's hand. "Interesting."

The blond man narrowed his eyes. "Really? That's all you've got to say after what you just did to us?!"

He removed a switchblade from his boot.

Sebastian stiffened when he felt the stranger's powers surge. He flexed his right hand, his own energy pooling in the center of the mark on his palm. The blond man's blade transformed into a sword that shimmered with a soft, white haze. The hairs rose on Sebastian's nape when he discerned the nature of the weapon the man now held.

He blinked, impressed despite himself. "Magnificent."

"I don't think this asshole is listening to us," the tall, dark-haired man said with a scowl.

Sebastian frowned as the knife in his hand transmuted into a sword, this one darker and edged with wicked teeth. He could sense a more sinister energy throbbing from the third man and his blade.

"You are the ones trespassing upon my property," Sebastian said coldly. "I demand to know what you—" A smell reached him. His eyes widened in horror. He raised a hand hastily to cover his mouth and nose. "Good Heavens! What *is* that evil miasma?!'

The intruders turned and stared at the hound.

"I get the feeling beans don't agree with him," the Dragon muttered.

"You think?" the dark-haired man said sardonically.

The dog disregarded them, his unblinking gaze locked on Sebastian. An eerie feeling snaked through Sebastian as he beheld the intelligent, dark eyes lit from within with a faint red light.

The blond man studied the hound with a frown. "Are you okay?"

Sebastian froze when a voice rang clearly inside his head. Though no one had spoken, he knew instinctively that it belonged to the dog.

Yes. I am sorry, I am just a little...surprised. I believe his powers are similar to ours.

The blond man and the dark-haired man startled, along with the Dragon. They could evidently hear the hound too. Sebastian's heart thudded against his ribs as they turned and assessed him with fresh stares.

The woman frowned, puzzled. "What's going on?"

The man with the glasses had gone pale.

"What was that voice?" he asked tremulously.

The blond man gazed at him, clearly surprised. "You can hear Smokey?"

The man blinked slowly, his round eyes moving to the hound. "That was Smokey?!"

"Yeah," the dark-haired man murmured, studying their shocked companion. "I guess that's the first time he's spoken in your presence."

"Smokey says he might be one of us," the Dragon told the woman, whose face had grown impatient.

She directed a suspicious look at Sebastian. "You sure about that? 'Cause the guy just attacked us."

The hound took several cautious steps toward Sebastian, snout up and sniffing the air.

Thump.

Heat flared inside Sebastian as the one who lived within him stirred and opened a lazy eye. A memory flashed before him. The same memory he could see reflected in the hound's shocked gaze.

The creature transformed into a chocolate-colored Rex rabbit in the next moment and leapt into the blond man's arms, his fur bristling and his body trembling.

"What's wrong with the pooch?" the woman asked, now utterly baffled.

"Smokey?" The blond man pressed a protective hand against the rabbit burrowing into his shirt. "What is it?"

The dark-haired man and the Dragon glared accusingly at Sebastian.

Sebastian paid them no heed, his mouth dry and his entire being focused on the creature in the blond man's arms. The creature who appeared to have recognized the beast within him. The creature he was experiencing the strangest affinity with.

He is…

The rabbit opened one eye and peeked anxiously at Sebastian.

—our brother!

Shocked silence fell around them.

"Huh?" the Dragon said.

Blood thrummed dully in Sebastian's ears as he felt the one within him rouse itself and peer curiously at their uninvited guests through his eyes.

Oh. At long last. They are finally here.

Before he could fathom the shocking words his beast had just uttered, an alarm started ringing around the library. Sebastian's pulse spiked as the shrill sound echoed against the walls.

He scowled at the intruders. "Please tell me you closed the barrier after you."

The blond man looked at him blankly. "I thought it closed itself."

"Curses!" Sebastian snarled. "They can sense the bookstore now!"

"Er, who can?" the blond man said, a guilty expression washing across his face for the first time.

"The demons, you cretin!"

CHAPTER SEVEN

THE MAN TURNED AND BOLTED ACROSS THE LIBRARY.

"He's a strange little guy, isn't he?" Serena murmured.

"I don't think I've ever heard anyone call someone a cretin before," Drake said.

"His clothes are weird," Otis added.

Haruki changed back into his human form and scratched his nose. "I suppose we should go after him."

Artemus sighed. "Well, considering the horde of demons I can feel approaching this place is apparently our fault, I think we kinda have to."

He could feel the corrupt energy building somewhere above them. There were definitely demons about. Smokey growled, leapt from Artemus's hold, and morphed back into his hellhound form, his powers surging as he too detected the growing threat.

They found the bookstore owner heading for an old-fashioned cage elevator in the west wall of the gallery.

Artemus stepped inside after him. "Mind if we tag along?"

The man whirled around, his expression accusing. "Haven't you done enough damage for one night?!"

"Look, we're sorry," Artemus said with an apologetic grimace while the others piled in after them. "We just wanted to talk to you. And your place wasn't exactly easy to find."

"There's a reason for that!" the man snapped. He grunted as everyone pressed closer to fit inside the elevator. "Well, is he coming or not?"

They all stared at the hellhound where he hesitated outside the metal cage.

Otis looked around their narrow confines. "Oh. I don't think he'll fit."

Smokey huffed irritably, changed back into his rabbit form, and hopped inside the elevator.

"Why a rabbit?"

The bookstore owner reached behind Drake with some difficulty and pressed a button, his ire dissipating for a moment in the face of his curiosity.

"It's the form of the pet he ate the first time I met him," Artemus replied.

The man made a face. "That sounds positively gruesome."

The elevator groaned and rattled as it started its ascent.

"Can this thing go any faster?" Serena asked after a moment.

The man narrowed his eyes at her. Now that they were no longer glowing, Artemus could see they were chestnut brown in color.

They finally reached what appeared to be the first floor of the bookstore and stepped out into a corridor. Weak light illuminated the passage from the gas lamps that lined it. Surprise filled Artemus when the man turned and waved a hand where the elevator stood. It vanished instantly from sight, taking on the appearance of the wall that surrounded it.

"You're gonna have to tell us how you did that," Artemus said pensively.

Although he could feel the man's energy signature faintly, a power that was identical to the one he'd sensed in the barrier he'd cut through with his sword, he still couldn't figure out what the guy's abilities were.

"I do not have to do anything of the sort, thank you very much," the man said coldly.

He headed briskly along the passageway. They followed.

Artemus was unsurprised to see that there were windows in the exterior walls of the building. By the looks of it, the bookstore owner had masked them like he had the elevator and his store.

Curiouser and curiouser.

"I'm Artemus Steele, by the way. This is Drake, Haruki, Serena, and Otis. The rabbit is Smokey, as you already know."

The man slowed a fraction ahead of him.

"Sebastian. Sebastian Theodore Dante Lancaster," he said gruffly.

Serena arched an eyebrow. "That's quite a mouthful. Can we call you Seb?"

Sebastian rocked to a halt and glowered at her. "No, you may not!"

"How about Theo?" Drake proposed.

"*No!*"

They entered the shop fronting the property. To Artemus's surprise, it was considerably bigger than it appeared from the outside and even boasted a mezzanine gallery.

"Dante?" Haruki hazarded.

Sebastian turned, his right hand glowing with a ball of crackling white light. "The next one who makes an idiotic suggestion gets this in the chops."

"Alright." Drake raised his hands defensively. "Take it easy, dude."

Sebastian grumbled an archaic curse under his breath, did something to the front door lock, and pulled the heavy panel open.

Demons were pouring through a narrow breach in the redbrick wall that faced the building, yellow pupils glowing in the night.

"Ooops," Artemus said with a sickly smile. He turned to Otis. "You should hang back for this."

Otis nodded, face ashen as he stared at the creatures crawling toward them.

Sebastian cast a dark look at Artemus. Both his hands were now alight with balls of pulsing, white energy. "I have to repair the barrier. I take it you can manage the demons?"

He glanced at their swords.

"Yes."

Artemus removed his stainless-steel gun from the rear waistband of his trousers and clasped his blade in a firm grip.

Sebastian studied the firearm with an intense stare.

Serena drew her daggers. "Sure thing, Sebbie."

"Whatever you say, Bas," Drake drawled, his watch extending into a shield.

Haruki grinned and morphed back into his Dragon beast. "Roger that, Ba-chin."

A faint snicker escaped Smokey where he stood next to Artemus, his form that of the black hellhound once more.

Sebastian scowled at Artemus, his eyes growing luminescent with power.

"I'm sorry. Their self-preservation instincts broke a long time ago," Artemus explained, contrite.

Unholy shrieks rose to the night sky as the demons charged.

CHAPTER EIGHT

DRAKE DECAPITATED THE FIRST TWO DEMONS, DUCKED beneath a set of deadly talons, and stabbed the third creature in the chest. Black blood burst from the demon's lips and dripped down his chin, his body taking on its human appearance as he sagged lifelessly on Drake's blade. Drake pushed the corpse off his weapon and clenched his teeth.

The foul energy churning the air was resonating with that of the devil inside him. He took a shallow breath and fought down the terrible bloodlust building in his veins.

It was growing much faster this time around. Every time he fought Ba'al, Drake sensed that he surrendered a part of himself to the demon who lived within him.

Artemus glanced at him. His brother was engaging a group of demons fifteen feet to his right, his bullets ripping fiery holes into their bodies before rendering them into exploding clouds of ash. Smokey tore a demon's throat up ahead, cast the body aside, and cast a quick look at Drake over his shoulder.

Drake could feel their anxiety thrumming through the thread that bound them.

The last time he'd gone all out with Ba'al, he'd lost control of his powers, stabbed Artemus in the arm, and almost attacked Callie and Haruki. It was thanks to his brother that he'd managed to subdue the monster inside him and imprison it behind the barricades he'd erected to protect himself from the fiend's corruption.

A mocking half-smile tilted his lips at that thought.

My soul is already defiled. I am as damned as the demon who sired me.

BONE CRUSHED UNDER SERENA'S ELBOW WHEN SHE thrust it into a demon's nose. The creature screeched, dark liquid spurting from his wound and splashing onto her jacket. She made a face, jumped back to avoid the claws headed for her abdomen, and kneed the demon in the groin.

The creature's eyes and legs crossed, his hands dropping protectively to his nether parts.

Serena slashed his neck with a blade and stepped around the dropping body. "Hey, has anyone noticed yet?"

"Noticed what?" Haruki said from her left. "Give me a minute!"

He took the legs out from under two demons with his tail and killed them where they fell, his flaming sword carving hissing wounds into their chests.

"The only way they're getting in is through the break in that wall."

Serena swooped beneath a blow directed at her head, roundhouse-kicked the demon who'd attacked her in the gut, and sent him flying. The creature sailed through the air before smashing into the bookstore frontage, his neck snapping with an audible crack. He slid to the ground, his body shifting to that of a human.

"Uh-oh," Serena muttered when she saw the crater the impact had left in the wall.

"*I saw that!*" Sebastian snarled from where he was fixing the wall Artemus had broken, one hand busy undoing the damage caused by the sword while he cast exploding lightning balls at the demons around him with the other.

"You're right." Artemus impaled a demon with his blade and examined their surroundings. "I can't see any rifts. And they're not appearing out of the darkness like they've done in the past."

Their gazes shifted to Sebastian.

"Does that mean his barrier extends all around this building?" Drake said quietly. "Like a bubble?"

"If it does, then that's the first time I've seen anything like it," Artemus said in a guarded tone.

It took another ten minutes to dispose of the remaining demons. By the time they'd finished, Sebastian had restored the wall and it looked as good as new once more. He dusted his hands, slipped his gloves on, and strolled toward them with a determined expression.

"Now, how about you young rascals explain what it is exactly you are here for?"

Haruki stared. "'Young'?"

Serena grimaced. "'Rascals?'"

"What century do you think this is?" Drake said dully.

"I am well aware of the date," Sebastian snapped. "And I *am* older than you."

"Okay, maybe by a couple of years," Artemus admitted grudgingly. He pursed his lips. "I bet you'd look younger if you dressed less stiffly."

"Try two centuries," Sebastian retorted coolly. "And my clothes are just dandy, thank you ever so much."

SEBASTIAN WATCHED SHOCK FLARE ON HIS UNINVITED guests' faces. He waited for the familiar guilt and regret to sweep over him. The same guilt and regret he'd lived with since the night he survived the demon's attack on his home, all those years ago.

The feelings came with their customary wave of bitterness and brought with them an echo of screams that made him clench his fists.

"Wait," Artemus said incredulously. "You're an Immortal?!"

Sebastian frowned. "If you mean I am afflicted with the curse of longevity, then the answer is yes."

"No." Serena's expression had turned wary. "He means a real Immortal. As in someone who can die up to seventeen times."

Surprise rushed through Sebastian at her words.

Artemus stared at Serena. "I didn't know there was a limit to the number of times they could be revived."

Serena hesitated. "There is, for most of them."

"So, the race really does exist," Sebastian mused. He stroked his chin thoughtfully. "I have never found physical evidence of their existence, so assumed they were but a myth."

Serena's face grew grim. "So, you *do* know about the Immortals."

"I have knowledge of many things, child," Sebastian said haughtily.

Her eyes grew chilly. "Did you just call me a child?"

"Now, let's all calm down," Artemus interjected in a pacifying tone. "I'm sure he didn't mean any—"

A vile stench filled the air.

They turned and saw Smokey urinating on the remains of the few dead demons that hadn't burst into ash. The creatures' corpses were disintegrating amidst rising, foul, acid vapors.

"What in the name of Heavens is he doing?" Sebastian said, aghast.

Artemus's expression turned apologetic. "It's kinda like his victory dance."

Sebastian clenched his jaw, marched across to the hellhound, and pointed a reprimanding finger in his face. "Stop that disgusting performance right this minute! You are being a disgrace!"

Artemus gaped.

"He's gonna lose that finger if he's not careful," Drake muttered.

"He's gonna lose the arm," Haruki said flatly.

Sebastian and Smokey glared at each other for a fraught moment.

There was a collective gasp from Artemus and his companions when the hellhound huffed, turned, and padded over to them, his body morphing into his rabbit shape along the way. He turned his furry butt deliberately to Sebastian and nibbled grumpily on Artemus's left boot.

Artemus stared from Smokey's sullen expression to Sebastian's self-satisfied one. "How the hell did you do that? He never listens to me!"

Sebastian sniffed. "I am his older brother. And I do believe I have chewed him out many a time when he was but a pup."

CHAPTER NINE

"You would like my assistance in translating copies of your mother's journals?"

Sebastian observed Otis with an impassive expression.

They were gathered in a parlor on the second floor of the bookstore, in Sebastian's private quarters. Despite the lateness of the hour, he had made them a fresh pot of tea and served it with left-over cake.

Not only did the guy dress and speak like someone from Victorian England, he most definitely acted that way too. Artemus studied the room they sat in with curious eyes.

He could tell just from looking that the antiques around them were authentic, including the exquisite bone china tea set their host had served their refreshments in and the couch and armchairs they sat on. If what Sebastian had told them about his age was correct, then the apartment spread over the top two floors of the bookstore would be a veritable treasure trove for any collector of period pieces.

And that doesn't even begin to include the rare books he has in the library beneath this building.

Although Artemus was itching to know more about the secret galleries hidden beneath them, Sebastian had so far been unforthcoming with information. He could tell the man still had his guard up despite the battle they'd just fought together.

If he was indeed related to Smokey and Callie, and Artemus didn't have any reason to doubt the hellhound's instinct on this matter, then that would make him a divine beast too. The term Daniel Delacourt had used to refer to Callie and Smokey.

As for the name of the supernatural creature who likely dwelled within him and was the source of his powers, Sebastian had yet to divulge its identity and Smokey seemed mysteriously none the wiser.

"Yes," Otis said in response to Sebastian's question. "They're written in a code I cannot decipher. The Vatican has dozens of experts who've pored over them, to no avail." He faltered. "I learned of you and your bookstore through someone I met on the internet and thought you might be able to help."

"That astonishes me, considering the bookstore is not advertised anywhere." Sebastian raised an eyebrow. "And truly? The Vatican?"

Artemus and the others exchanged cautious glances.

"What do you know about Ba'al?" Artemus said.

A blank look washed across Sebastian's face. "Who is Ba'al?"

They stared at him.

"It's the name of the demons' organization," Serena said. "You know, the same demons who just attacked your bookstore?"

Sebastian ignored Serena's slightly supercilious tone. A muscle jumped in his cheek as he digested what she'd just said, his eyes darkening with a nameless emotion.

"So, their name is Ba'al."

"You didn't know?" Artemus said, surprised.

Sebastian did not meet his eyes. "No, I did not."

"But you knew about the demons' existence," Haruki said, puzzled. "And how to fight them."

"When you have lived as long as I have and witnessed the things I have had the misfortune to observe, demons hardly come as a surprise, boy."

Artemus narrowed his eyes. He was beginning to suspect that Sebastian liked to speak in riddles when he wanted to avoid a subject that troubled him. He decided a direct approach would get them answers faster.

"Are you a Guardian?"

⁓

SEBASTIAN FROWNED. "WHAT IS A GUARDIAN?"

Artemus and his friends gazed at him with surprise.

"Wow, you really have no idea, do you?" Serena murmured.

Sebastian bristled. "I will have you know that I am knowledgeable on many matters, young lady."

Serena's expression grew cool.

"Did he just call you a lady?" Haruki said out of the corner of his mouth.

She cut her eyes to him.

Sebastian clasped his gloved hands together to stop from fidgeting. He had loaned Haruki one of his dress shirts and was dismayed to observe how hideously it clashed with the rest of the man's outfit, which consisted of modern designer jeans and boots. The words his father had spoken to him when he was a mere child of five years echoed inside his head.

"Sebastian, my dear boy, a gentleman owes it to himself and to society to be well-dressed for every occasion."

It was a doctrine Sebastian had adhered to even after his family was murdered by the first demon he ever encountered, on that cold winter's night one hundred and eighty-two years ago.

It had been the weekend after his tenth birthday celebration, an extravagant affair engineered by his mother and his two sisters and which had involved inviting half the county's high society to their estate, much to his everlasting horror. Though he had scolded them for the lavish do, Sebastian knew they had done it out of love for him, and to try and get him out of the funk he had fallen into of late.

Sebastian had been at great pains to conceal his distress at the recurrent nightmare he had been experiencing that month. Evidently, he had not been truly successful at it. The dream had been so fantastical that he knew it would only shock and worry his family if he were to reveal the details to them. And so, he had kept it a secret.

To this day, Sebastian wondered if disclosing the particulars of the nightmare, to his father at least, would have saved his family from their ghastly fate on that terrible night. The only light in the absolute darkness that had been that incident was that half their servants had been saved from the brutal killing, his parents having generously given them leave to recompense them for their hard work the previous week.

It had taken him a long time to understand what had

happened in his bedroom when he had faced the monster who had murdered his family. In the moment that the demon had charged toward him to deliver what would undoubtedly have been a fatal blow, the most incredible feeling of power had exploded inside him and brought forth a blinding sphere of light in his right palm. A sphere he had instinctively cast at the demon.

He would never forget the creature's shriek of rage and agony in the seconds that had followed, nor the black blood that had gushed from the terrible wound his attack had inflicted upon it. For the ball of light had cleaved one of the demon's arms and part of its face clean off.

After staggering about for a moment, the demon had gathered its severed limb and leapt through one of the bedroom windows, one eye glaring balefully at Sebastian before it vanished into the night.

Heedless of the shards of broken glass scattered across the floor of his bedroom, Sebastian had rushed over to the sill and watched it land two stories below before bounding for the woods that surrounded the estate.

After a long and insufferable investigation, the authorities in the county and in London had concluded that a large animal of indeterminate breed had broken into the mansion and savaged his family, even going so far as to point an accusing finger at a travelling circus that had been visiting the city at the time.

Sebastian had listened to this verdict stoically when he was apprised of the news. Nothing would ever bring back his family and telling the police about the creatures from his nightmare would only see him committed to an asylum.

Since he was still a minor, Sebastian's care and the management of the fortune and lands he had inherited were entrusted to the only relative he had, a distant aunt on his father's side whom he had never met and who resided in London. Much to his relief, the elderly lady was made of the same mettle as his father and had given him the kind of upbringing his own parents would have aspired to for him.

It was during his formative years at Eton and subsequently at the various famous colleges he attended that Sebastian realized the night of his family's murder had changed him in more ways than one. For he discovered that he had developed an almost insatiable hunger for knowledge, one that he had not possessed before. Not only that, he proved to be incredibly talented at languages and was able to speak and write fluent Latin, German, French, Spanish, and Cantonese by the age of sixteen, a skill that brought him offers from many distinguished learning institutions in England and Europe in the years that followed.

Deep down inside, Sebastian recognized that his abilities were not natural and that they were born of the one that lived inside him. The creature who had awakened the night of the demon's attack.

The monster who had saved him and cursed him in equal measure to a most wretched fate.

CHAPTER TEN

"THREE MONTHS AGO, A WOMAN NAMED CALLIE STONE brought a silver and gold-plated ivory walking cane to Chicago, to be sold to the highest bidder at a private function held at an auction house," Artemus said quietly. "The artifact had originally been purchased by her now deceased husband, Ronald Stone, in a thrift store in Jerusalem a couple of decades previously. The cane turned out to be the Scepter of Gabriel and the key to a gate of Hell. Callie Stone is the manifestation of the divine beast who guards that gate, which took the form of a stone arch excavated by Ba'al in Jerusalem around the same time Ronald came across the cane." He paused. "She is the Chimera and Smokey's sister."

Shock reverberated through Sebastian as Artemus's words echoed around him.

"Ba'al stole the Scepter and kidnapped Callie and one of our friends in an attempt to force her to open the gate," Serena said. "We stopped them before they could do so."

The look in her eyes told Sebastian she was being less than generous with the truth.

"Three weeks after we defeated Ba'al in New York, their activities increased in L.A," Drake said. "At the origin of the incidents was the murder of Yashiro Kuroda, the heir to the Kuroda Group." He glanced at Haruki, who now wore a pained expression. "Yashiro was Haruki's older brother. Not only did he discover Haruki's key in the form of a bracelet he purchased for his younger brother on the other side of the world, he also came across another portal to Hell, this one in the shape of a mirror. Haruki's divine beast is the Colchian Dragon and he is the Guardian of the second gate. The weapon you saw his bracelet transform into is the Flaming Sword of Camael."

Blood thundered dully in Sebastian's skull. Though he wanted to disbelieve the people seated in his parlor, to deny the fantastical things they were telling him, he could not do so. For every word they uttered resonated keenly with the creature inside him.

"Our second battle with Ba'al was a close one," Artemus continued, his gaze growing troubled and distant as he relived memories of the skirmish. "It was in L.A. that we came to learn more about the demons' hierarchy and what they are truly capable of. New York fooled us into thinking they might be weak." His face turned hard. "They are anything but."

"The demon in charge of the L.A. branch of Ba'al called himself Asmodee," Drake added grimly. "He was—"

"A Prince of Hell," Sebastian interrupted, his mouth now dry. "Or a sub-Prince, to be precise."

Otis brightened. "You know of The Book of Abramelin?"

"And the *Pseudomonarchia Daemonum*," Sebastian murmured. "I have an original copy of both publications in my personal library." He ignored the excitement dawning on the young man's face and turned to Artemus. "The only thing I never managed to discover, despite all my inquiries over the decades, was the identity of the demons roaming the Earth."

"It was in Otis's mother's journals that his father first identified the name of the organization they belong to," Artemus said.

Astonishment coursed through Sebastian. He observed Otis with renewed interest. "Was your mother also possessed by a supernatural entity?"

An uncomfortable silence fell upon them.

"Yes," Otis replied. The animation in his eyes had been replaced by remorse and pain. "Me."

Sebastian stared.

"That is most odd," he said after a while. "From all appearances, you are the only normal person in this room. I am not detecting anything unusual from you and neither is the beast inside me."

"Who is your beast, by the way?" Artemus asked curiously. "Smokey doesn't seem to be able to recall the name right now."

The frustration that had been Sebastian's constant companion nearly his entire lifetime surfaced with a vengeance.

He frowned. "I do not know his name."

They stared.

"Though I have been his host for one hundred and eighty-two years, the boorish cad has yet to reveal his identity," Sebastian elaborated in tones of utter disgust.

"What?" Artemus breathed.

Deep inside his soul, Sebastian thought he sensed the beast smirk. His frown deepened. He realized the others were looking at him as if he had grown two heads and a tail.

"You first met your beast in—" Artemus faltered, lines marring his brow as he made the mental calculation.

"Eighteen fifty-seven," Serena muttered.

"Thanks." Artemus studied Sebastian intently. "Are you certain?"

"Unwaveringly so," Sebastian stated flatly.

Drake appeared equally stupefied by Sebastian's assertion. He looked at Artemus. "That means—"

"Everything we ever assumed about our awakening was wrong," Artemus finished.

It was Sebastian's turn to be puzzled.

"Our powers all manifested themselves for the first time on the night of August 14th, twenty-two years ago," Artemus explained. "They brought with them permanent marks inked into our skin."

Sebastian kept his face carefully blank. He was conscious of his gloved hands where they rested on his thighs and what the coverings concealed.

"It was seven months later that the first demon sighting recognized by the Vatican took place, in Turin," Artemus added.

"Ah," Sebastian murmured. "The incident at the cathedral."

Artemus did a double take. "You know about that?"

Sebastian dipped his chin. "I do. But I am afraid the creature who possessed that teacher was not the first demon. Not by any stretch of the imagination. Demons have been around for much longer." His tone turned cold. "Even longer than the one who killed my family."

CHAPTER ELEVEN

CALLIE OPENED HER EYES WHEN SHE HEARD A VEHICLE approaching the house. She gazed at the sky above the estate before rising from the ornate metal swing on the rear porch and heading back inside the mansion, her mind as muddled as it had been all night and most of that morning.

The others were piling through the door when she entered the foyer.

"You think he'll come?" Serena asked dubiously.

"He said he would," Artemus replied.

"What's stopping him from closing up shop and disappearing on us?" Drake said, looking equally unconvinced. "Or making a stronger barrier so we can never find his bookstore again?"

"They're right, you know," Haruki muttered.

Artemus sighed. "The three of you really need to work on your trust issues."

They turned when they heard her approach. Smokey's eyes lit up. He hopped across the checkered tiles and leapt joyously into her arms. Callie buried her face in his fur as he settled against her chest with a contented rumble.

"You're back," Artemus said, surprised.

Callie nodded. "I came home a day early."

Serena watched her for a moment. "From the dark circles under your eyes, I take it Nate confessed?"

Callie's heart sank.

"Oh, wow," Haruki said. "Is that what he meant yesterday, when he said he wanted to talk to her?"

"Yeah," Serena murmured.

"Kudos to the big guy," Drake drawled.

A choked noise made them look around.

Artemus was gaping at Callie. "Wait, Nate did what?!"

"Nate likes Callie," Serena said.

Callie groaned and began to wish the ground would open up and swallow her whole. She could feel her face burning nearly as badly as when Nate had admitted harboring romantic feelings for her last night.

Artemus opened and closed his mouth soundlessly. "And you all knew?!"

"Well, yeah, genius." Serena shrugged. "I mean, Callie was oblivious, as always."

"Hey!" Callie protested weakly.

"I thought you would have picked up on it at least, but it turns out you're as much of an idiot as she is," Serena told Artemus blithely.

"Don't be hard on him," Haruki said. "He doesn't have much luck when it comes to affairs of the heart."

Artemus narrowed his eyes at the Yakuza heir.

"So, you turned him down?" Drake asked Callie.

Callie chewed her lower lip.

"Not exactly," she admitted in a small voice.

Serena frowned. "What do you mean?"

Callie hesitated in the face of the super soldier's accusing stare. "I said I would think about it."

Serena's face hardened. "If you mean to refuse him, I would rather you do it sooner rather than later."

She turned and headed up the main staircase, her back stiff.

"What's her problem?" Haruki murmured.

Guilt twisted through Callie as she watched Serena disappear. The thing was, Nate's confession had taken her completely by surprise.

A warm friendship had blossomed between them after what they had gone through together at the hands of Ba'al in New York. Callie knew Nate had felt protective of her since, despite the fact that she was more powerful than him in her beast form. Their relationship was one that brought her comfort in much the same way as her bonds with the others did and she knew Nate would readily put his life on the line for her, as she would for him.

Though she sometimes flirted teasingly with Artemus and Haruki, Callie had never once considered the super soldier in a romantic light. From Nate's expression last night, he had not held high hopes that she would return his affections and had evidently resigned himself to being rejected even before he spoke up.

Yet, Callie hadn't been able to say no. She had sensed her beast's interest when Nate had confessed and had expected her to voice an opinion on the matter. To her surprise, the Chimera had remained silent. From what Callie could feel from her, it seemed she was content to leave this particular decision in Callie's hands.

Smokey's voice echoed inside Callie's head, distracting her from her jumbled thoughts. Her eyes widened when she registered what he'd just said. She stared at Artemus, Drake, and Haruki.

"Wait. You met our older brother?!"

Artemus grimaced. "It's a long story."

~

SEBASTIAN CAST A FINAL LOOK AT THE FIRE BEFORE retracing his steps to the first floor of his home, satisfied that his preparations would last a while. He finished packing, headed through the bookstore, and stepped out into the cool morning air.

Dawn was filling the horizon to the west with red light. The remains of the dead demons who had fallen outside had long since dissipated, their ashes scattered by the winds blowing off the sea.

Sebastian put his luggage down and turned to press a hand against the lock on the front door. Light glowed around his fingers as he strengthened the barrier that was already there, sparks of power spreading out over the wood to cover the facade of the building. His home shimmered for a moment, the energy flowing out of him resonating with bricks and mortar. He stepped back, examined the place with a critical eye, declared himself satisfied, and picked up his baggage. He was at the exterior wall that surrounded the property in seconds and walked through as if it were thin air.

A cat startled when he appeared at the end of the dingy alley. It observed him from large, yellow-rimmed pupils and let out a low rumbling purr when he walked over and leaned down to scratch its head gently. The cat licked Sebastian's fingers before washing its paw and turning to disappear up the gloomy passage, its tail swinging sinuously.

The alleyway was different to the one Artemus and his friends had travelled to find his shop three days ago. It was sheer luck, or more likely providence, that the building had been at that particular location that night. For his bookstore had not one but five different addresses in Salem.

Sebastian knew Artemus and the others had been hugely curious about his powers when they'd left his home, after he'd promised to come to Chicago to help Otis Boone translate his mother's journals. If he had to give his abilities a name that people would understand, then it would be magic. But it was more than that. So much more.

Truth be told, Sebastian was wealthy enough not to have to engage in any kind of labor or employment. That he chose to do so was out of sheer boredom. A man could only take so much leisure time before slowly going out of his mind with the monotony of it. As such, the bookstore was seldom open to the public and he reserved his opening hours for the rare occasions when one of his contacts in the world of collectible books decided to pay him a visit.

It was inevitable in this day and age that rumors would eventually spread about his shop. And if humans could uncover his whereabouts, then so could demons. Which was why Sebastian had taken to moving the bookstore to a new locale every week.

The people of Salem seemed largely oblivious to the fact that a three-story building had been appearing and vanishing from various sites throughout their town for the last six decades.

As for how he could achieve such a wondrous undertaking, only his beast knew, the ability to manipulate space seemingly being part of his powers, as was the talent of inducing what appeared to be some kind of amnesia in the minds of the few humans who had ever stumbled across his secret.

Sebastian cast a final longing look at the brick wall that hid his home from curious eyes. He loathed leaving the place for any stretch of time, even when he travelled the world looking for unusual volumes to add to his private collection. Were it not for the fact that Artemus and his friends had piqued his interest and appeared to know more about the demons than he did, he would have refused their request for assistance.

He heaved a sigh, walked to the end of the alley, and climbed inside the town car waiting for him. The driver closed the door after him and proceeded to load his luggage into the trunk.

They reached the airport north of the town shortly and pulled up to a private jet waiting on the tarmac.

Sebastian greeted his pilot with his customary reserved nod. "Good morning, Harry."

The pilot ignored his formal greeting and grinned jovially. "And where are we off to today, sir?"

"Chicago."

Sebastian headed up the steps, took a last look at the encroaching daylight, and entered the plane.

Emblazoned in bold colors on the door of the aircraft was his family crest, a golden lion on a field of red.

CHAPTER TWELVE

THE FRONT DOOR OF THE DETACHED TOWNHOUSE opened to reveal Elton in a smart evening suit.

Artemus stared. "I thought the dress code for this thing was casual."

A murmur of low conversation rose from somewhere behind Elton.

He frowned. "The invite specifically said black tie."

"It did?"

Artemus retrieved the invitation card he'd gotten in the mail yesterday and that he'd immediately stuck in the interior pocket of his windbreaker.

The thing came out half-chewed and dribbling with drool.

All eyes shifted to the rabbit at the end of the leather and silver chain Artemus was holding loosely in one hand. Smokey's nose twitched, his expression radiating pure innocence. Artemus gave him a dark look and wiped his hand on the back of his jeans.

Elton sighed as he studied their less than fashionable attire. The only ones wearing anything remotely smart were Callie, whose summer dress and handbag matched Smokey's leash, and Nate, who was sporting a stylish navy blazer over cream chinos.

"You might as well come in," he grumbled. "Just try not to do or say anything embarrassing. The mayor's here."

Artemus's heart sank at that piece of news. He loathed formal parties with a passion and disliked having to engage perfect strangers in polite conversation. It was bad enough that Elton forced him to attend these kinds of functions when he held one of the closed-door auctions he was famed for, Artemus usually being the one responsible for finding the rare and valuable objects that were put up for sale at those events. He headed reluctantly after his mentor, grateful that he'd convinced the others to accompany him.

Elton's home was a short distance from his auction house in Lincoln Park and a leisurely walk from Artemus's antique shop in Old Town. Set over three stories, the pretty limestone building with its mansard roof fitted in perfectly with its pricey neighborhood. It was one of the many properties Charles LeBlanc, the forefather of the LeBlanc dynasty, had owned when Chicago was still a flourishing nineteenth century settlement.

Elton guided them through the foyer and down a hall to a sizeable drawing room that opened onto a formal dining area overlooking the rear gardens. A pair of beautiful crystal chandeliers suspended from the ornate ceiling cast a dazzling light on the crowd circulating beneath them.

"This is a small gathering?" Artemus said glumly as he eyed the thirty or so stylishly attired guests milling about the place.

An amused smile curved Drake's lips. "You really hate parties, don't you?"

"Yeah."

Artemus spied Isabelle and Mark by the grand piano next to a bay window and headed over to them, Smokey hopping beside him.

"Hey, Art. Hi, Fuzzface." Isabelle glanced at the figures trailing in their wake. "Wow. The whole team's here, huh?"

Callie studied the two Immortals curiously. "Are you guys here on official duty?"

"Elton insisted, since the mayor was attending." Mark inspected their clothes with a puzzled look. "Did you guys not get the invite?"

"The least said on that subject, the better," Artemus muttered.

Smokey let out a sheepish huff next to him.

"I'll go get us some drinks," Callie said, her expression preoccupied.

Haruki exchanged a glance with the rest of them. "I'll come with you."

Since there were waiters walking around with trays of champagne and party food, Artemus could only hazard one guess as to why Callie had overlooked them in her distraction.

No one could fail to sense the tension that had grown between her and Nate in the last few days. The strange thing was that, as far as Artemus could see, Nate's behavior had not changed in the least. He still treated Callie the same way he had always done and spoke to her in the calm, measured tones he used with everyone else.

It was Callie who seemed more on edge.

It didn't take long for Artemus to realize their group was drawing inquisitive stares. He stiffened when he registered the morbid interest dawning on the faces of many of Elton's guests. He suspected it had as much to do with the fact that he was holding a rabbit on a leash as it did with Callie's reputation as the widow of one of the richest men in the country and Haruki's notoriety as a Yakuza heir.

A feverish buzz started in the drawing room and soon spilled through the rest of the crowd. Artemus frowned. Elton had disappeared somewhere and was bound to be oblivious to the speculation building amongst his guests. He hoped his old friend would not regret having invited them tonight. He knew Elton was anxious to talk to him in more detail about what he'd revealed to him concerning their recent trip to Salem and what they had discovered there.

"I don't think you need to worry about Callie and Haruki," Drake murmured.

Artemus followed his brother's gaze to where the pair were getting drinks and plates of food from a table set against the dining room wall. Callie and Haruki were taking the increasingly avid looks being directed at them in their stride.

Serena grabbed a glass of champagne from a waiter. "Since when does Elton socialize with the mayor?"

"Since forever." Isabelle made a face. "By the way, be careful around that guy. His hands tend to stray when he's tipsy."

A middle-aged man was looking at Serena admiringly from where he stood talking in the midst of a flock of people next to the fireplace.

Serena returned his interested stare with a cold one. "Is that him?"

"Yup," Isabelle muttered. "That's Loose Finger Joe."

"Now, don't you go do anything rash," Artemus warned

at Serena's expression. "Elton will kill me if we hurt one of his guests."

"Define rash," Serena said.

Artemus turned to Nate. "Talk to her, will you?"

"If he touches you or Callie, I'll break his arm," Nate told Serena.

Artemus swore.

"Language," someone growled behind him.

Artemus turned and saw Elton approaching with an attractive blonde at his side. Helen Tempest looked much more youthful than her age would suggest and had warm, twinkling eyes that Artemus immediately liked.

"You forgot to mention that your protégé was such a handsome young man," Helen told Elton teasingly. She took Artemus's hand and pressed a soft kiss to his cheek. "Hello, I'm Helen. It's a pleasure to finally meet you."

Artemus felt his ears grow warm. "Oh. Er, hi. I'm Artemus."

"He does have more than a five-word vocabulary," Drake said drily.

Helen chuckled. Elton made the introductions just as Callie and Haruki returned.

Helen studied their group with a curious tilt of her head. "I do believe your arrival is causing quite the commotion."

A wary look appeared on Elton's face as he finally registered the restless atmosphere now hanging over the room.

"Sorry," Artemus muttered. "I didn't realize our coming here would turn your party into a circus."

"Nonsense," Elton retorted. "If I hadn't wanted you here, I wouldn't have invited you in the first place." He grimaced. "I had hoped more formal attire would help you blend in, but I suspect you guys would stand out whatever you were wearing."

"He's right," Helen told a startled Artemus. "Individually, you are all quite striking. But as a group, I have to admit you come across as somewhat...dangerous." She glanced at Smokey. "Well, except for him. He's just adorable."

Elton gave them a guarded look. They all knew Smokey was not in the least bit cute in his hellhound form.

The doorbell rang.

"Oh." Helen's face brightened. "That might be him."

Elton excused himself and headed out to the foyer.

"Are you expecting more guests?" Callie said politely.

"Yes. A colleague from Oxford is visiting the city. He's delivering the keynote address at a conference at the university next week." Helen smiled. "He seemed most interested in meeting Elton."

Elton returned with three men in tow. Two of them were built like tanks, their identical suits indicating they were bodyguards of sorts. Their faces were curiously blank. But it was the third man who made the most striking impression of the new arrivals.

Tall and thin, he bore a shock of white hair that he'd tied in a queue that hung between his shoulder blades. A faint scar was visible on his left forehead and cheek, around the eyepatch that he wore. His right eye was cobalt blue in color and filled with an intense light.

CHAPTER THIRTEEN

"THIS IS PROFESSOR JACOB CUNNINGHAM," HELEN SAID.

She went around their group and made introductions.

Serena studied Elton's new visitors with a carefully neutral expression. Though Nate also maintained a blank face beside her, she could tell he was trying hard not to stare at the two men with the professor. She caught Drake's puzzled glance and ignored it.

Cunningham's grip was firm when he shook Serena's hand.

"A pleasure," he murmured, his smile polite.

"And this is Artemus Steele," Helen finished, "Elton's former ward."

Cunningham's face visibly brightened. He clasped a startled Artemus's hand in an enthusiastic gesture. "Oh. Even better!" He looked apologetically at Elton. "I expressed a keen interest in meeting you when Professor Tempest informed me that you were an acquaintance of hers. Had I known I would be crossing paths with the world-renowned Artemus Steele as well, I would have brought something more substantial from my cellar to express my gratitude."

He gestured to one of the men with him. The guy silently whipped out a bottle of wine from inside his jacket and presented it to Elton.

Elton's eyes widened as he accepted the gift. "You shouldn't have."

Serena could tell from his expression that the vintage was worth a lot of money.

"I'm afraid I'm at a loss to understand your fascination with us," Elton said, exchanging a bemused glance with Artemus. "I cannot quite see why a theology professor would be so interested in what we do." His gaze moved to the silent men standing watch behind Cunningham. "Or need bodyguards, for that matter."

Cunningham's mouth twisted in a contrite grimace. "Oh. Do forgive my forwardness. And on the contrary, your work is of great importance to me. I am very fond of antiques and have quite the collection myself." He waved a dismissive hand at his silent guards. "As for my escort, I am afraid the field of theology can occasionally prove hazardous to one's health, what with all the religious zealots out there. There have been several threats issued against my person these past two years and the college insisted on taking measures to protect me."

A business-like look washed across Elton's face. "Did you wish to make a purchase while you were in Chicago?"

Cunningham laughed. "Alas, no. I suspect most of the items for sale in your auction house are well outside my price range. I do, however, have an object that I wish for you to look at." His gaze shifted to Artemus. "Well, actually, I was hoping Mr. Steele would be able to give me his opinion on it too."

"What is it?" Elton said, intrigued.

Artemus frowned faintly.

"It's a book. One that I have had in my possession for a while." Cunningham smiled. "I would like to know its origin. I also require assistance with its translation."

DRAKE WATCHED SERENA EXCUSE HERSELF AND WANDER off, on her way to the restroom. He waited a moment before stepping away and following her. Nate stayed with their group, silent and face devoid of emotion.

Though they were trying their best not to show it, Drake could tell the two super soldiers were on their guard. Something had spooked them.

Drake was unsurprised to see Serena walk past a restroom and head through the kitchen and out the back door into the gardens. He lost her for a moment when she negotiated a short flight of stairs and vanished into the shadows. A soft light punctuated the darkness behind a large hydrangea bush to the left. He headed toward it.

A faint murmur reached him as he drew near. Serena was calling someone on her smartband.

Drake slowed, conscious he was eavesdropping.

"Gideon? I've found them," Serena said in a low voice.

Even from a distance, Drake heard the person on the other end of the call inhale sharply.

"Are you sure?" a man said, his tone harsh.

"Positive," Serena replied. "Two of them are in Chicago right now, on bodyguard duty for a visiting theology professor from Oxford."

There was a short, tense silence.

"You think you or Nate could put a tracker on them?" the man finally asked, a hint of hope coloring his words.

"I'm going to pretend you didn't just say something that stupid." Serena paused. "Gideon? I have to go." She ended the call, stepped around the hydrangea, and narrowed her eyes at Drake. "How much did you hear?"

Drake shrugged. "Pretty much all of it. So, who are those guys with Cunningham?"

Serena hesitated. Drake frowned and folded his arms across his chest. She sighed.

"They are first-generation super soldiers."

Drake stared. He recalled what she'd told them in New York several months ago, about the super soldier experiments and Jonah Krondike, the Immortal who had spearheaded the illegal program that spanned several decades, all with the blessing of a rogue faction of the U.S. military.

"I thought you said they were rehabilitated. Something about chemical lobotomization."

"Some were. Many weren't. Those super soldiers who couldn't be reformed to integrate into human society were kept in secure facilities known only to the U.S. President and the Immortals."

Unease wound through Drake at her words. "Were? You used the past tense."

Serena watched him guardedly. "Three years ago, one of those facilities was attacked and some one hundred of the first-generation super soldiers escaped. Neither we nor the Immortals know the identity of the group who launched that assault."

Drake digested this for a silent moment. "You said 'we.'" He frowned. "Are you and the other super soldiers from Greenland trying to track down the whereabouts of your predecessors?"

Even though it was night, he saw a muscle jump in Serena's jawline.

"Yes. They are incredibly dangerous. And they have no filters. They are mindless machines whose entire purpose for existing is to wreak havoc and death on those around them. They will do the bidding of whoever controls them, blindly, with no respect for property or innocent lives."

Drake studied Serena broodingly. He'd seen her, Nate, and their other super soldier friends in battle mode in New York and knew how deadly they could be, even against demons. The fact that they were worried about the first generation of their kind spoke volumes about the abilities of the latter.

"Is this Gideon your leader?"

Serena grimaced. "Not really. But he is the smartest of all of us. He's the one coordinating our efforts to find the missing super soldiers."

"We should tell the others about this," Drake said.

Serena's eyes grew chilly. "This is none of your business. It concerns me and Nate only."

Drake gave her a grim look. "It *is* our business. Like it or not, you and Nate are part of our weird, dysfunctional little family. And it feels as if these super soldiers turning up now might not just be a coincidence."

He turned and started making his way back to the party. Serena wavered before following him.

"So, if we're a family, does that make Artemus our dad and Callie our mom?" she said after a short silence.

Though she spoke lightly, Drake could tell that his words had affected her. He'd long suspected Serena and Nate felt like outsiders in their team, since they didn't possess his and the others' unnatural abilities. He knew

Artemus, Callie, Smokey, and Haruki didn't personally feel that way about the pair, and neither did he.

"Technically speaking, I'm older than Artemus. And Callie is younger than all of us bar Otis. So, I should be the dad and you the mom."

They stopped and stared at each other in frozen silence.

"Let's drop this conversation," Serena said dully.

"Yes, let's," Drake muttered.

CHAPTER FOURTEEN

CALLIE SAT IN THE BACK IN SILENCE AS SERENA DROVE past the park and headed up the private road that appeared shortly after on the left. Thin clouds drifted across the crescent moon sitting in the sky above the low hill ahead. The mansion's wrought-iron gates appeared in the SUV's headlights a moment later.

It was gone eleven and they'd just left Elton's party. Though she was normally fond of Elton's company and liked his new girlfriend, Callie was relieved they'd taken their leave. She was edgy enough as it was without having to suffer the curious stares of Elton's other guests.

She glanced at Serena in the driver's seat. It would normally have been Nate who would have driven, but he had disappeared before they left the reception. When questioned about it, Serena had been vague, murmuring that something urgent had come up and that he'd be home shortly.

It was evident to everyone that she was being sparing with the truth and Callie had noted Drake's pointed frown as he'd stared at the super soldier.

Callie swallowed a sigh. Though Nate had continued to treat her the same way as ever in the days since his confession, she could not help but feel irritated. The fact that she couldn't really explain why she felt this way only served to vex her more.

Artemus stiffened where he sat next to Serena. "Did you guys leave the lights on?"

They had just cleared the trees. The mansion appeared on the rise, its eldritch spires and chimneystacks stark against the moonlit sky. The windows on the first floor were bright, radiant rectangles, their glow spilling onto the garden that fronted the property.

"No," Drake said quietly.

Serena dimmed the headlights and stepped on the brakes. The vehicle lurched to a stop some hundred feet from the mansion.

"I'm not sensing demons," Callie murmured.

"And thieves wouldn't announce their visit so blatantly," Haruki said.

Artemus frowned. "Still, let's be careful."

They left the vehicle and moved cautiously toward the house, Smokey morphing into his hellhound form as he padded on the grass next to Callie.

It was Haruki who found their visitor in the mansion's formal drawing room. He turned to them with a disconcerted expression as they converged on his location, Artemus frowning briefly at the suitcases next to him.

"You're not going to believe this," the Yakuza heir murmured to Artemus, cocking a thumb over his shoulder.

Callie stared at the elegantly dressed man he was indicating.

The stranger was seated in the Queen Anne chair next to the fireplace. He put the dainty porcelain cup he had been drinking out of on the saucer on the side table, wiped his mouth fastidiously with a napkin, and looked pointedly at the Black Forest clock on the mantelpiece.

"What kind of ungodly time do you call this?" he asked Artemus coldly.

The rest of them crowded in the doorway.

Thump.

Callie startled as the Chimera stirred inside her. She could feel something from their unexpected visitor. He rose to his feet and adjusted his bottle-green vest and cream cravat, faint lines wrinkling his brow.

Something uncanny.

The stranger's gaze landed on her.

"Oh. Do forgive my manners." He closed the distance to Callie, took her hand in his gloved one, and bowed slightly to press a kiss on the back of her fingers. "Sebastian Theodore Dante Lancaster, at your service."

Trepidation filled Callie at the name.

Thump-thump.

Her eyes widened when she finally recognized the energy thrumming against her skin. She caught a glimpse of Smokey darting behind Artemus, his shape that of a rabbit once more. The hellhound's nervousness hummed along the thread that bound them.

Callie could hardly blame him.

"Hey, how come I didn't get the special kiss-the-hand treatment when we first met?" Serena said testily.

Sebastian straightened and arched a supercilious eyebrow at the super soldier, his hand still wrapped around Callie's. "Because you, my dear, do not in the least bit act like a noblewoman. I dare say you have the foulest mouth of any female of my acquaintance and your fighting tactics are somewhat dishonorable. Striking a man in his private parts is most boorish."

Haruki bit his lip. Drake looked at his feet, his shoulders shaking slightly. Serena opened and closed her mouth soundlessly.

It was the first time Callie had seen the super soldier lost for words.

"They were *demons*!" Serena finally blurted out.

Sebastian ignored her and turned to Callie, his expression charitable and clearly oblivious to her mounting horror. "This fine gentlewoman here, on the other hand, is the very definition of a young mademoiselle."

"Oh, really?" Drake said. "That young mademoiselle is Callie Stone, the Chimera. Apparently, your sister."

Sebastian let go of Callie's hand so fast it fell limply to her side and struck her thigh with a faint slap. "Oh."

A look of passionate disgust dawned on his face.

"*Oh God!*" Callie groaned. "It is you, isn't it?"

The Chimera gazed contemptuously at her older brother through Callie's eyes.

Artemus stared at Sebastian. "How the hell did you get in here?" He pointed at the cake on the coffee table. "And did you bake while we were out?!"

"We were at a friend's house," Artemus said.

Sebastian observed his host where the latter leaned against the kitchen counter. The others were gathered around the table that dominated the homely room and were demolishing the cream cake he'd made in their absence, Serena still wearing a somewhat surly mien. Callie and Smokey were watching him with similarly sour expressions while they chewed and swallowed.

"This is the best thing I've ever put in my mouth," Haruki said with a heartfelt sigh, polishing his fork with fervent enthusiasm. He glanced guiltily at the figure opposite him. "Except for your pancakes, obviously."

"It's good cake," Nate admitted reluctantly.

The man had just turned up. From what Sebastian could sense from him, he likely shared the same superhuman abilities as Serena.

"So, how did you get in?" Artemus repeated, puzzled. "Did you climb over the wall?"

"Don't be absurd. I came through the gates." Sebastian took a sip of freshly brewed coffee and stared at Nate. "This is quite delicious."

Nate overlooked his faintly accusing tone and dipped his chin magnanimously. "Thank you. I roast and grind the beans myself."

"You will have to tell me the name of your supplier," Sebastian murmured.

Artemus sighed. "It's great that you guys are exchanging recipes, but the gates have an access code. One that isn't easy to decipher." He paused, his tone turning sardonic. "Let me guess. You used whatever that power of yours is and magicked the damn things open."

Sebastian eyed him coldly. "I would prefer it if you stopped comparing my abilities to those of a fool performing conjuring tricks at a child's birthday party. And I am frankly surprised at your reaction. All I did was make a doorway in the barrier around this property. Incidentally, I would very much like to meet the person who created it. It is quite formidable."

Silence descended on the room.

"What barrier?' Artemus asked, his eyes round.

Sebastian could tell the surprise resonating around the kitchen was genuine.

"There is a protective barrier surrounding this estate," he said slowly. "Are you honestly not aware of it?"

Artemus exchanged shocked glances with the others. "No!"

Sebastian hesitated. "I can show you, if you wish. The conditions are ideal right now."

There were general nods all round, each face filling with curiosity.

Sebastian led the way out the back door and into the garden. He stopped on the lawn that edged onto the private cemetery sitting within the grounds of the estate.

"I would stand back if I were you."

"Why?" Artemus said suspiciously. "What are you going to do?"

"Make an explosion."

Sebastian removed the glove on his right hand, looked up at the sky, and drew on the power of the creature within him.

Heat danced through his veins and pooled in his palm. A glowing ball of energy flared into life in his hand, the light pulsing faintly with his own heartbeat and that of his beast.

It never ceased to amaze Sebastian how perfectly matched he and the creature were during these moments. And how gloriously righteous the power he wielded felt, despite his misgivings about the circumstances under which they had become associates and the malediction of his immortality.

"Are you sure about—?" Artemus started.

Sebastian ignored him, drew his arm back, and cast the sphere at the sky.

It accelerated against the odds as it gained altitude, its tail flaring like that of a comet.

"Here it comes," Sebastian murmured.

The sphere exploded with a bright flash some two hundred feet above their heads, the resulting thump booming against their eardrums.

Artemus inhaled sharply as the remains of the lightning ball sparked across an invisible structure, the dying particles radiating in every direction to reveal the dome-like form of the intangible energy barrier that encased the estate.

"Whoa," Haruki murmured. "That's incredible."

Serena and Nate were gazing at the sky, their faces ashen.

"What is it?" Drake asked worriedly.

Serena swallowed and glanced at Nate.

"We've—" she faltered, visibly shaken, "we've seen something like this before. When we were children. It was the night we were rescued from the facility in Greenland."

"You mean, the night all our powers awakened?" Artemus said, clearly stunned.

Serena nodded, her expression turning grim.

Sebastian frowned. Though he did not know what they were talking about, he sensed it was of importance. He could not deny that he grew more intrigued with every moment he spent in the company of these people.

He wasn't sure if this was a good or a bad thing.

"From what I can sense about this barrier, its main purpose is to prevent demons from detecting your whereabouts and entering your land."

Sebastian moved toward Artemus, his hand glowing with power once more.

Drake narrowed his eyes and stepped forward. "Hey, what are you—?"

Sebastian raised his hand a foot from Artemus's chest and trailed his fingers gently through the empty air.

There were gasps all around as light flashed across an invisible wall.

"This barrier is not just around your property," Sebastian told a shocked Artemus. "It's around all of you. Protecting you. Shielding you." His gaze shifted to the astonished group watching him. "But it is strongest around *you*." He stared at Artemus once more before looking at Drake. "And you." He pulled his glove back on. "It obviously cannot stop a direct attack. That is not its purpose. No, whoever created this was determined to mask your auras from demons during your day to day activities. And they appear to have done a pretty good job of it."

Sebastian checked the time on the antique pocket watch hanging inside his vest, turned, and headed back toward the mansion.

"Come now, children. The hour is late and we must retire to our beds." He stopped and looked over his shoulder at where they still stood, staring after him. "Speaking of which, I have determined that the chamber on the second floor with the elaborate cast-iron fireplace surround and the dual-aspect windows is most to my liking."

"This guy's high and mighty attitude is starting to piss me off," Serena muttered darkly.

"I hear you," Callie mumbled.

Artemus scowled at him. "That's my room! And who the hell said you could stay?!"

CHAPTER FIFTEEN

"Have a good day."

Artemus's smile faded when the customer left the shop, the miniature painting she'd just purchased tucked under her arm. He sighed, glanced at the grandfather clock opposite the counter, and rubbed the back of his neck with a wince.

One hour to go, then I can close up.

It had been three days since Sebastian and Otis had confined themselves to Otis's apartment, busy poring over the copies of the journals that had belonged to Catherine Boone. From what Artemus had been able to deduce from the scant words he'd exchanged with the pair, they were close to some kind of breakthrough.

This meant he was doing double duty, having had to take over Otis's role in the front of the shop as well as working on the costly pieces commissioned by clients in his workshop out back.

He had hoped the others might be able to help, but they'd all left to go their separate ways that morning with suspicious hastiness, Haruki to L.A. for a meeting with the

Triad, Callie to San Francisco on business, and Drake to somewhere he wouldn't reveal, which made Artemus highly doubtful that whatever his twin was engaged in was legal. Serena had flown to Mexico the previous day on some secret mission. As for Nate, Artemus hadn't seen much of him lately either.

Artemus recalled the conversation he'd had with Elton two days ago. Elton had been as shocked as he had been to discover that there was some kind of protective wall around the LeBlanc estate. From what Sebastian had told Artemus the morning after he arrived in Chicago, it had been there for many years.

"There's one around Karl's shop too," Artemus had told Elton quietly. "Sebastian detected it when he first came to see Otis. It's weaker than the one at the mansion though. He said something damaged the barrier a while back and it was never repaired."

The second troubling topic he'd discussed with Elton was what Drake had revealed to him about Serena's suspicions concerning the men who had accompanied Jacob Cunningham to the party. The super soldier had declined to discuss the subject when Artemus had broached it with her, insisting that it was up to her and her super soldier friends to address the matter.

Drake had disagreed and so had Artemus.

"Tell Isabelle and Mark," Artemus had said to Elton. "I suspect their bosses are going to want to know about this."

"I will," Elton had replied in a grim voice. "Incidentally, I spoke to the Vatican about what your guy in Salem said concerning demons having been around for a while. They were most intrigued. They very much want to meet him."

Artemus had grimaced. "I seriously doubt you're going

to convince Sebastian to go to Rome. That guy is an ornery bastard and does as he pleases."

"Really?" Elton had drawled. "He's in good company then."

Artemus had scowled at that.

"There's something else," Elton had added. "The Vatican have insisted that we not interfere with the super soldiers or the Immortals."

Artemus had stiffened at that. "Why?"

"They wouldn't say."

"Do they disapprove of Serena and Nate being with us?"

Elton had sighed. "They didn't exactly say that either."

"Well, if they do, tell them they can stuff their objections where the sun doesn't shine," Artemus had stated coldly. "Serena and Nate are part of our group. The only way I see them leaving is if they do so of their own free will, not because some douchebag in Rome dictates it."

He'd practically heard Elton wince at the other end of the line.

"I don't think the Pope would appreciate being called a douchebag."

Elton had ended the call with a promise to keep Artemus updated with any further developments.

A sound made Artemus look down.

Smokey was snoozing in a wicker basket Otis had prepared for him for the occasions when the rabbit got bored watching Artemus in the workshop and decided to hang out with him out front. His hind leg was currently beating the air while he dreamt of God only knew what.

Artemus observed him wryly. *Probably kicking the shit out of demons.*

"Some help you are."

Smokey opened one eye, gazed at him lazily, and yawned.

The bell above the shop entrance rang.

Artemus looked up and stared at the man who had just entered the building. "Oh. I'm sorry. I'd forgotten about our appointment."

Jacob Cunningham smiled. "That's quite alright. I'm just pleased the shop is still open. Is this a good time?"

There was a small package wrapped in oilskin in his hand.

Artemus glanced at the two figures who came in behind Cunningham. "Sure."

∾

OTIS STARED AT SEBASTIAN. "SO, YOU'RE SAYING THERE are Enochian sub-dialects?"

Sebastian rubbed his chin thoughtfully. He stilled when he felt the rough stubble on his skin. It was unlike him not to be impeccably groomed at all times. He was astonished that he did not feel more discomfited.

Then again, these are unusual times.

He glanced around the room they sat in. Practically every surface, including the floor and walls, was covered in paper. Otis had even purchased free-standing white boards which now formed a ring around the couch. They were covered in Sebastian's elegant, flowing handwriting and Otis's less than graceful penmanship.

"I believe so," Sebastian said. "We just need to figure out the glyphs that mark the hidden alphabets. That should help us create a map with which to translate your mother's writings."

Otis's eyes shone with excitement despite the dark

circles beneath them. They had been working almost without rest for three days, Sebastian leaving the apartment only to sleep and have supper at Artemus's mansion.

In all his years searching for information about the identity and purpose of the demons whom he knew walked among mankind, Sebastian had never felt as close to an answer as he did now. Otis had shown him the sections of his mother's journals that his father had managed to translate and what they had revealed about an upcoming Apocalypse, as well as Artemus and Drake's roles in it.

Sebastian had been brooding over this ever since. For Catherine Boone's journals had revealed something else. Something perturbing.

She had written about beasts. About creatures who would play as important a role in the forthcoming Judgement Day as Artemus and Drake. Sebastian knew instinctively that the monster inside him was one of those beasts. Just like the ones who lived inside Callie, Smokey, and Haruki. According to Catherine Boone's predictions, there were other beasts too.

A strange feeling suddenly swept over Sebastian. His skin prickled, as if an icy wind had passed over him. He stiffened, confused by what he was sensing.

Anxious lines wrinkled Otis's brow. "Hey, are you okay? You look really pale all of a sudden."

Sebastian's stomach lurched when he finally grasped what his subconscious had just recognized. He got up from the couch, strode rapidly to a window that overlooked the road outside the antique shop, and tugged his gloves off.

"Sebastian?" Otis mumbled, rising to his feet.

Sebastian's heart slammed against his ribs. He pressed his right hand to the glass.

"*Reveal*," he whispered.

Warmth flared on the mark on his palm. Tendrils of energy sparked outward from his flesh, breaching the window and snaking through the air outside. He made contact with the barrier around the shop and clenched his jaw.

Demons!

Sebastian twisted on his heels and stormed toward the apartment's exit.

"Whatever happens, do not leave this room!" he barked at Otis.

CHAPTER SIXTEEN

"GREAT." CUNNINGHAM CROSSED THE SHOP FLOOR. "IS there somewhere more private where we can examine the book?"

Artemus was aware of Smokey having risen next to him. The rabbit was standing quite still, his attention focused on their guests even though he could only see their shoes under the counter.

He could sense the hellhound's puzzlement and shared it.

Cunningham's aura came across as human. Still, Artemus couldn't shake the feeling that something wasn't quite right about the man. Judging from Smokey's demeanor, his instincts appeared to be right on the money. As for the bodyguards with the professor, Artemus now recognized the faint energy signature emanating from them. After living with Serena and Nate, he knew it was nanorobots he was sensing.

There was also a strange smell. It was faint and sulfurous, reminding Artemus of rotten eggs.

"Let's go to my office. I was thinking of closing shop soon anyway."

He stepped around the counter and went to put the closed sign on the door under the watchful gaze of Cunningham's escort. The professor observed Smokey with an amused expression as the rabbit hopped by Artemus's side.

"He is rather precious. I never did catch his name at the party."

"It's Smokey," Artemus murmured. "Follow me."

The bodyguards stayed on their heels as he showed Cunningham to the corridor that led to the rear of the building. He entered his office ahead of the men and walked over to the Victorian oak pedestal desk that took pride of place in the room.

The professor studied the antique admiringly. "An original, I take it?"

"Yes." Artemus took the chair behind the desk and indicated the one on the opposite side. "Please, take a seat."

"Thank you."

Cunningham sat down and laid the package he was holding on the table. He undid the wrapping almost reverently before taking out what lay inside.

It was a slim tome covered in black leather and bearing a red iron clasp.

"From the verses within, we believe it to be a book of poetry. We discovered it in Croatia two years ago, but we feel its origin might be somewhere entirely different."

Artemus reached across and picked up the book. He arched an eyebrow. "'We'?"

Cunningham smiled apologetically. "I belong to a book club that specializes in dissecting rare finds. It was one of my associates who stumbled across this tome when he was visiting the country. He discovered it in an abandoned church, in a village in the Velebit Mountains."

A frown marred Artemus's brow as he examined the volume. Smokey jumped onto his lap and sniffed the leather curiously. Artemus undid the clasp and slowly leafed through the thick, yellow pages covered in cursive script.

He could feel little from the book. That in itself was unusual.

There was a reason why he was one of the best antique and rare goods valuers in the world, albeit one whose skills were never openly celebrated. Not only could he tell the authenticity, age, and origin of an item with his senses, he could also detect if it was an object of power, or one that was cursed by evil.

"Do you think you can help?" Cunningham said.

"I don't know," Artemus murmured. "I—"

"*Get away from him!*" someone roared.

Smokey jumped slightly in Artemus's lap. Artemus looked past Cunningham and his guards to the man in the doorway of his office, startled.

Sebastian stood glaring at them, his eyes glowing with power and his body braced for an attack. A ball of lightning sparked and crackled in his right hand.

Surprise washed across Cunningham's face. "Oh." He rose and turned, the smell of rotting eggs intensifying around him. "What a pity. I did not think my identity would be unmasked so soon, but it appears I was mistaken."

∾

THUMP.

Sebastian's world spun dizzily as he stared at the figure before Artemus's desk.

Thump-thump.

The man smiled. He reached up and removed the leather patch covering his left eye.

Sebastian's heart pounded violently when he saw the sea of obsidian that filled the empty orb, its center carved by a vertical slit of repulsive, yellow light. Though the creature looked like a man, Sebastian knew him. Would have known him even if he were deaf and blind. The scent was unmistakable.

Impossible. It cannot be!

"Why, if it isn't little Sebastian," the demon drawled in a mocking voice, his human appearance dissipating as his body assumed the nature of the monster that lived within him. He grew by several feet, his skin darkening to a filthy shade of black. "It's been a long time, my dear earl." He fingered the terrible scar on his face. "I believe I owe you something in return for the gift that you gave me on the night we first met."

Goosebumps broke out across Sebastian's skin. A wave of revulsion washed over him. He searched the office frantically with his gaze. Something else in the room was resonating negatively with him and his beast. Something dangerous. Dread wormed its way into Sebastian's veins.

He'd experienced this aura once before.

A suffocating feeling robbed him of his breath, scattering his thoughts. He choked as an evil miasma suffused the room and filled his lungs.

He could see Artemus and Smokey struggling where they stood behind the desk, the rabbit a hellhound once more and Artemus holding his pale sword in one hand. Their eyes glazed over and they started to sway.

Sebastian gritted his teeth and cast the sphere of energy in his hand. It flashed across the room, twisting in fast arcs that destroyed the foul vapor wreathing the chamber in thick, oily currents. Heat flooded his lungs, clearing his passages of the toxic fumes that were dulling his senses. He could feel his beast behind his eyes now. The creature was fully roused, his anger fairly roiling through Sebastian's bones.

Artemus gasped as he finally drew a breath of clean air. Smokey wheezed and shook his head dazedly beside him.

The demon ignored them and observed Sebastian like a scientist would a lab rat it wanted to dissect. "How interesting. I see your powers have grown."

"Artemus?" Sebastian said between gritted teeth.

"Yeah?"

"This is the demon who murdered my family."

Artemus's eyes widened. A low growl rumbled out of Smokey. The hellhound's pupils flashed red and his lips peeled back, exposing his fangs.

Movement drew their attention to the two men who had accompanied the demon. Shudders were coursing through the pair, as if they were in the grip of violent spasms. Surprise shot through Sebastian.

He was sensing the same strange aura from them that he'd detected the first time he'd met Serena and Nate. But there was something else beneath it. Something dark and twisted.

Artemus cursed as the men's limbs lengthened, their fingers and toes extending to form talons that shone with a metallic gleam, the claws shredding their shoes as if they were made from paper.

"The hell?" Artemus said. "These guys are demons too?!"

The watch inside Sebastian's left breast pocket started to tremble, startling him. Up ahead, the men were still transforming, their already massive bodies swelling to gargantuan proportions until their heads almost touched the ceiling, their eyes mutating into odd, liquid-silver films split by yellow centers.

There was a moment of breathless stillness.

The demons moved.

CHAPTER SEVENTEEN

SMOKEY SPRUNG TOWARD THE CREATURE TEARING IN their direction. The demon blurred and vanished. The hellhound smashed into a filing cabinet with a grunt and sent it toppling to the floor.

Something slammed into Artemus's stomach with the force of a sledgehammer. He gasped and doubled over, his grip loosening on his sword. An iron fist closed around his throat.

Artemus choked and struggled as he was lifted effortlessly into the air, talons slicing hot lines into his skin where the demon grasped him.

The creature was standing in front of him. Though his features and body were those of a monster, his expression remained chillingly blank.

How the hell is he moving so fast?!

There was no more time to think. The demon tightened his hold on Artemus's neck and drew his other arm back, his claws elongating until they resembled six-inch knives evidently intended to rip him to shreds. Black spots clouded Artemus's vision as the creature squeezed his windpipe. He scowled and tapped into the power inside him, the wing marks on his back trembling violently. The demon struck.

Metal shrieked and sparks erupted.

The demon stared at the sword Artemus had used to block his attack a hairbreadth from impact. The blade was longer and broader, its surface dancing with flashes of gold and silver.

Artemus drew his knees up and kicked the demon violently in the gut at the same time he swung the sword up, slicing through the creature's wrist. The demon smashed into the desk, cleaving it nearly in half, black blood spraying from his cleanly severed stump.

The creature's hand thudded to the ground in front of Artemus as he landed on the floor. He glared from the mangled remains of his favorite bureau to the demon rising awkwardly to his feet.

"Oh, now I'm *seriously* pissed!"

On the other side of the room, Smokey's eyes flared from red to liquid gold, his body expanding as he faced the second super soldier demon. Blood was dripping from a set of shallow cuts on his black hide, where the creature had landed a blow. From the corridor outside came flashes of light and loud bangs as Sebastian engaged Cunningham.

Movement brought Artemus's gaze to the demon before him. His eyes widened as the creature sprouted a new hand, pale bones and grisly flesh knitting together with seamless speed as they snapped and cracked into existence, streams of what looked like liquid silver flowing along newly formed veins and nerves.

The demon flexed his new appendage slowly before looking at Artemus, his face still vacant.

SEBASTIAN DREW A SHARP BREATH AS A SET OF TALONS curved toward his face. A draft kissed his skin when he jumped back, the claws missing their mark by a hair-breadth.

"Not bad," the demon drawled. "And here I thought you would be pissing yourself in terror, like you did last time."

Sebastian clenched his jaw, power pooling in his right hand as he glared at the monster towering over him.

"I am no longer a child, you sack of excrement!"

The pocket watch inside his vest was now vibrating alarmingly, the metal growing hotter against his flesh with each passing second.

Curses! Why is it doing that?!

Sebastian glimpsed motion below. He grabbed the demon's hand a moment before the creature's clawed fingers could punch through his ribcage and crush his heart. Surprise gleamed in the obsidian eyes opposite him.

Sebastian bared his teeth. Light bloomed around his fingers as he drew on his power. The demon frowned at the smell of his own burning flesh, his dark gaze dropping to the white lines snaking across his skin, their edges tinged with the redness of charring meat.

Something glinted to Sebastian's left. Heat flared on his forearm, drawing a gasp of pain from his lips.

A thin, gray rope had just wrapped around his limb. It glinted and writhed as if it were alive, its surface dancing like molten metal. Sebastian followed the cable to the demon's right hand. His eyes widened.

It was growing out of the creature's very flesh, its thick end protruding from his wrist bones as if it were an extra appendage. Sebastian stiffened when he sensed the odd aura that he associated with Serena and Nate coming from the weapon.

"Do you like it?" The demon smirked. "It's a new toy of mine."

Sebastian bit down on his lip as the rope tightened around his forearm, ripping his sleeve to shreds and flaying his skin.

Take the watch.

Sebastian blinked.

"Why, I could snap your bones with a twist of my little finger," the demon taunted. "Maybe I should do that to all your limbs." He paused, his macabre smile widening. "Or better still, how about I rip your friends' heads clean off their bodies before I kill you?"

The beast inside Sebastian scowled.

Let go of his hand and take the watch!

This time, Sebastian obeyed instinctively. The antique warmed his skin as he snatched it from his breast pocket. It transformed in his grip with his next heartbeat, the metal glowing as it lengthened into a long, shiny lash, its braids as smooth and as lissome as silk.

Sebastian and the demon stared at the golden whip.

The demon frowned. "Is that a—?"

Sebastian snapped the weapon. It whistled through the air and cleaved the cable holding his left arm prisoner, its movement sinuous and deadly.

He did not know how he had immediately grasped how to use it. Or why it felt like it belonged in his hand. Just like the day he'd come across the pocket watch, all those years ago.

The demon observed the shattered remains of the rope dangling from his wrist with a thoughtful expression.

Sebastian stared as it sprouted anew, metal shining with a sinister light along its growing length.

The demon sneered. "Let's dance, shall we?"

He flicked the rope.

Had it not been for the power resonating through Sebastian, he would have missed the lightning-fast movement of the weapon as it arced toward his legs. He jumped and cracked his own whip, the demon's rope flicking the air a few inches beneath his feet.

The golden lash glowed as it found the demon's left ankle, gouging a deep line into his flesh. The demon glared at Sebastian.

Sparks flashed and glinted as they moved along the passage, their weapons carving the air with faint hums while they launched blisteringly rapid attacks on one another, their lashes scorching dark grooves into the walls and ceiling of the corridor.

Blood thundered in Sebastian's veins as the unearthly energy inside him swelled and multiplied, his very bones trembling with the righteous fury of the beast within.

He had never felt this level of insane strength before.

The mark on his left palm, the one that had never manifested any sign of power, was growing warm. And there was an almighty itching between his shoulder blades and at his tailbone.

He landed a blow on the demon's face and another on his shoulder.

The creature backed toward the stairs, his face full of rage, black blood dripping from his wounds.

CHAPTER EIGHTEEN

ARTEMUS SWUNG HIS BLADE. THE SUPER SOLDIER DEMON blocked it an inch from his neck, the sword clanging against his rock-solid flesh. Across the way, Smokey closed his fangs on the second demon's thigh and tried to tear into him, to no avail. He growled and released the undamaged limb before backing away to a safe distance, the demon's leg intact where he'd bitten into it.

The office was a mess around them, paper from filing cabinets and his bureau strewn across the floor, some stained with Smokey's blood and the demons' darker ichor. Artemus panted slightly as he observed the blank-faced creatures, his heart racing from the intense fighting.

They are learning. The nanorobots inside them are adapting to our attacks!

Smokey's voice echoed inside his head, confirming his suspicion.

I believe you are correct. They smell more like machines than demons right now.

Artemus frowned. There could be no other explanation. By all accounts, these two demons should have been dead by now. He clenched his teeth.

His gun was in a drawer under the shop's counter. Even if he had it with him, he suspected the weapon would be ineffective against the super soldier demons' abilities.

Oh well, angel form it is then.

Artemus reached inside himself and drew on the untamed power that dwelled within his soul. Heat exploded through his body. His wing marks shivered as they prepared to unfurl.

Smokey shifted, his own body quivering as he braced himself to adopt his ultimate form as the three-headed Cerberus.

Running footsteps came from the corridor. Two figures flashed into view, their feet skidding as they drew to an abrupt halt in the doorway.

Even though their faces were concealed by masks that encased their heads, Artemus recognized the flat discs on their chests and the nanorobot, liquid-armor suits that covered their bodies.

"Get ready to deliver the final blow!" the smaller of the two figures shouted.

The larger figure removed a globe the size of a golf ball from the pouch at his waist, depressed the switch atop it, and dropped it on the floor. The demons stared at the device as it rolled to a stop in the middle of the room.

There was a faint whoomph. The air shivered, pressing uncomfortably against Artemus's eardrums.

The demons dropped to the floor, the light going out of their eyes.

"Now, dammit!" Serena snarled.

Artemus raised his blade and cleaved the first demon's neck. This time, his sword carved effortlessly through the creature's flesh. Smokey closed his fangs on the second demon's throat and ripped his head clean off. The creature's skull dropped from his jaws and thumped dully to the ground.

A hush fell over the room.

Nate walked in and stepped over the bodies of the dead demons. He retrieved the strange metal ball before peeling the mask off his face.

A crash sounded from upstairs.

Serena removed her mask and stared grimly at the ceiling. "Is that Cunningham?"

Artemus's stomach lurched. "Otis!"

SEBASTIAN GLOWERED AT THE DEMON WHERE THEY faced each other in the middle of the apartment.

Otis was crouched by the window to the demon's left, paper still fluttering around him from the explosion they'd created when they'd burst inside the room, his face ashen and his eyes wide with fear.

The demon glared at Sebastian. The metal rope growing out of his right hand had vanished a moment ago. Sebastian had sensed something from the room beneath them in the second before it had disappeared. A detonation of some kind.

He hesitated. Attacking the demon when the latter was so close to Otis risked the young man being caught in the crossfire. Otis's gaze moved to the golden whip in Sebastian's grip.

"Sebastian?" he mumbled hoarsely.

Sebastian realized Otis was clutching several of his

mother's journals to his chest. Motion drew his attention back to the demon.

The creature was staring at something on the floor. Astonishment flooded his face.

Sebastian followed his gaze.

The demon was studying one of Catherine Boone's journals where it had fallen open at his feet. He looked up and registered the white boards around them and the papers taped to the walls. He turned and scrutinized Otis with an intense stare.

No!

Sebastian moved before he was even aware he needed to do so. He snapped the golden whip. It missed its mark. The beast inside him growled in fury.

The demon was already at Otis's side.

Artemus's assistant gasped as the creature wrapped an arm around his waist and leapt toward the window.

"*No!*" Sebastian roared.

His voice was drowned out by the sound of breaking glass.

Sebastian stumbled to a stop in front of the jagged opening and watched in dismay as the demon landed smoothly on the street some twenty feet below, his hostage under his arm. Startled shouts echoed from the few bystanders who had witnessed the leap.

The demon looked up at Sebastian and crossed the road, a mocking sneer on his face. A rift burst open just beyond the barrier that protected the shop. Otis started struggling in the demon's hold when he saw the ghastly crimson light pulsing out of the portal.

The demon stopped and breathed out a foul miasma over his prisoner's face. Otis choked, his hands rising feebly to his throat. He went limp in the demon's grasp. They disappeared inside the rift.

Blood thundered in Sebastian's ears as he watched the portal close after them.

"Where is he?!" someone shouted behind him.

He turned.

Artemus stood in the apartment doorway, his sword in hand. He rushed inside the room ahead of Smokey, Serena, and Nate. His footsteps slowed when he saw Sebastian's expression. The blood drained from his face.

"Is he—?"

"No." Sebastian's grip tightened on the whip. "He is alive. The demon took him."

Raised voices came from the first floor of the shop. Someone yelled out Artemus's name. Drake, Haruki, and Callie charged into the apartment a moment later, their weapons in hand and their bodies vibrating with tension. They stumbled to a halt in the middle of the floor, their anxious gazes shifting from the mess around them to where Artemus and Sebastian stood by the window.

"What happened?" Drake asked Serena grimly.

A muscle jumped in her cheek. "We were too late."

"That's new," Haruki murmured.

Sebastian realized they were staring at the weapon in his hand. A weak cry outside drew his gaze. The putrid cloud the demon had released still pervaded the air and was slowly incapacitating the humans in the street below.

He flexed his fingers, drew a sphere of energy into his palm, and cast it at the thick vapor. It dissipated, its languid coils growing thin and indistinct until it was no more.

CHAPTER NINETEEN

"I FOUND IT AT A FAIR IN SALEM, IN 1970."

Haruki looked from Sebastian to the pocket watch on the kitchen table.

Having discovered no trace of Cunningham or Otis following the battle at the antique shop in Old Town an hour ago, they had returned to the mansion in gloomy silence.

The people who had accidentally witnessed the climax of the fight between Sebastian and Cunningham, and who had almost succumbed to the demon's noxious fumes, had woken up moments after the fact with no recollection of what had happened. Though no one had questioned Sebastian on the matter yet, Haruki and the others suspected the bookstore owner had had something to do with their convenient bout of amnesia.

"And you didn't know what it was?" Elton asked Sebastian doggedly.

He had come to the house at Artemus's behest. Isabelle had accompanied him, likely because Artemus had mentioned the super soldier demons he and Sebastian had just fought.

Smokey sprang onto the table from where he sat on Artemus's lap and sniffed carefully at the pocket watch. Sebastian frowned when the rabbit tentatively licked the antique.

"All I remember is the instant pull I felt toward it. It resonated strongly with my beast too." He looked up gratefully at Nate when the super soldier handed him a coffee. "Thank you."

Though Sebastian was doing his best to appear calm, it was clear to Haruki that his encounter with Cunningham had rattled him.

I can't exactly blame him. From what Artemus said, Cunningham's the one who murdered his family.

Haruki thought of his own dead brother and the demon who had callously taken his life several months ago, in L.A. Though he had slayed his brother's killer, the pain of that loss still echoed inside him every day. He couldn't imagine living with it for one hundred and eighty years.

"Cunningham called you an earl," Artemus said, his voice faintly accusing.

Sebastian's expression grew weary. "You are not going to let that go, are you?"

"No."

Callie's eyes rounded. "What?" She looked from Sebastian to Artemus. "You mean, he's like—related to royalty?!"

Sebastian shifted uncomfortably when he became the focus of a battery of morbidly curious stares.

"Yes, I am an earl," he admitted grudgingly. "And yes, I am related to the current monarchs of England, in a somewhat distant fashion."

"Wow. A real earl," Isabelle muttered in the ensuing hush. "I haven't met one of them in a while."

"No wonder he's a pompous ass," Drake murmured to Serena. "It must be genetic."

The super soldier grinned. Sebastian narrowed his eyes at them over his cup.

Haruki glanced at Sebastian's gloves. "Your marks. They are on your hands, aren't they? That's why you keep them covered all the time."

A guilty look flashed on Sebastian's face. He put his drink down and made to move his hands under the table.

"Wait up," Artemus said in a hard voice. "We've shown you ours. It's about time we saw yours."

Sebastian looked like he might balk for a moment. He hesitated, blew out a sigh, and finally tugged the leather coverings off his hands. They all leaned in to take a closer look.

There was a lion's head imprinted on his right palm in plain, dark lines. On his left was an eagle with a snake's tail.

Haruki stared. *I wonder what his beast is.*

The dragon stirred curiously inside him. *Whatever he is, he is rather powerful.*

Haruki grew thoughtful. *You can sense him too?*

The dragon yawned. *I can.*

Haruki faltered. *Is he...stronger than you?*

The dragon froze before bristling. *I did* not *say that!*

Haruki swallowed a sigh. Somehow, he suspected he had just mortally offended the divine creature living inside him.

"Your power. It only manifests in your right hand at the moment, correct?" Artemus asked Sebastian with a frown.

Sebastian dipped his chin, clearly puzzled.

"And you said you don't know the identity of your beast?" Artemus insisted.

"I already told you that he would not reveal his true name to me."

"You know, there's a good chance he doesn't know himself what he is yet," Haruki mused.

The others looked at him curiously.

"What do you mean?" Sebastian said.

It was Callie's turn to look pensive. "I agree with Haruki."

Sebastian narrowed his eyes. "You are not making this any clearer."

"Haruki and I did not know the names of our respective beasts until our gates were unsealed," Callie explained. "Not only that, our keys did not manifest their ultimate weapon form until that time too."

Sebastian froze. His expression grew shuttered. "You opened your gates?"

Haruki frowned slightly at his reaction. "Only partially. Callie's cane and my sword manifested sigils when we were faced with our gates. It wasn't until our beasts translated the divine symbols that they unlocked."

Sebastian brooded over this in the silence that followed. Haruki couldn't help but feel that this information both startled and troubled the bookstore owner.

"It's clear that the pocket watch is your key. That's why your beast was attracted to it, and, by default, you." Artemus reached out and lifted the antique in his hand. "I think the reason I can't pick up anything from it is because of you."

A guarded look replaced the disquiet in Sebastian's eyes.

"What do you mean?" Elton said warily.

"It's the barrier Sebastian created around his home and himself to protect his location from demons. It also shields this artifact." Artemus gazed steadily at Sebastian. "And I think I know how you generate it now. I finally figured it out when we were fighting Cunningham and his super soldier demons."

Callie's eyes widened. "You did?"

Artemus did not look away from Sebastian. "It's divine energy, isn't it? You can manipulate it."

Haruki stared, the shock coursing through him reflected on the others' faces.

Sebastian clenched his jaw.

Artemus ignored the man's displeased expression and placed the pocket watch on the table. "You might as well tell us. We *are* your allies."

The look on Sebastian's face indicated that this statement did not exactly fill him with confidence.

"You are correct," he grunted after a long pause.

Elton stiffened as a spark of light flickered into existence above Sebastian's right palm. Isabelle tensed where she stood beside him.

Neither of them had seen what Sebastian could do before.

CHAPTER TWENTY

"MOST PEOPLE THESE DAYS WOULD CALL THIS MAGIC. IN ancient times, my power would likely have been labelled as witchcraft." The spark flared and crackled in Sebastian's hand, growing larger until it became a bright pulsing sphere. "But, like you say, it is divine energy." He glanced at Artemus. "It took some time for me to figure this out myself. And to discover that our world is filled with it." He paused. "Why, I do not know."

His fingers twitched. The ball levitated slowly into the air.

"*Reveal*," Sebastian murmured.

There was a faint whoomph.

The hairs rose on Serena's arms. She straightened in her seat.

A thin cloud of glowing energy had burst into life overhead, filling the room from wall to wall.

"This house, though?" Sebastian gazed broodingly around the kitchen. "Well, you could say it is fairly saturated with it."

"Jesus," Isabelle muttered, face pale as she stared at the eerie phenomenon.

"You can say that again," Elton mumbled.

Serena observed Sebastian warily.

This guy's abilities are on a whole other level.

Sebastian closed his hand. The mantle of divine energy vanished as quickly as it had appeared.

"It must be because we're here." Drake exchanged a startled glance with Artemus before looking over at Callie, Haruki, and Smokey. "That's probably why there's so much of this—this divine energy around."

"It would explain why the barrier around this mansion is so strong," Artemus said pensively.

Sebastian dipped his chin. "I believe you may be correct."

Serena arched an eyebrow, incredulous. "Wait a minute. Are you guys saying you're leaking some kind of—" she waved a hand vaguely, "I don't know, divine body juice or something?"

Callie wrinkled her nose. "Well, when you put it like that—"

"It sounds kinda gross," Haruki concluded with a grimace.

"It's unsanitary is what it is," Nate mumbled, ashen-faced.

Serena bit back a sigh. Nate was a total clean freak and had once scrubbed an entire stall in a restaurant's restroom in Mexico before he would even dare use it, much to Lou and Tom's everlasting amusement.

"It's okay." Haruki patted Nate on the back. "I doubt we've infected you."

"I wouldn't bet on that, Dragon boy," Sebastian muttered.

Serena's pulse skittered at the look on his face. "What do you mean by that?"

Sebastian studied her and Nate for a moment. "Those minute machines inside you? The nanorobots? They are imbued with divine essence. As is your blood."

Nate's eyes widened.

Serena's mouth went dry. "How—how is that possible?!"

Sebastian shrugged at their stunned expressions.

"That I do not know. But I sensed it back in Salem." He gazed at Serena. "One of the demons inflicted a cut on the back of your left hand during our fight. I smelled it on your wound before it healed." He frowned faintly. "I do not know what level of power you possessed before but, surely, you must have realized this too. That you are stronger. As strong as the men who were with Cunningham today."

Nate looked as taken aback as she felt at that declaration. But the thing was, Serena could not very well deny it. She knew she was different now. And so did Nate. They'd noticed it when they fought the demons in L.A.

"Hey, does this mean Elton and I have this divine whatchamacallit too?" Isabelle asked. "I mean, we've known Goldilocks here since he was practically in nappies."

Artemus scowled. "I told you not to call me that. And we met when I was twenty-four!"

"I am afraid not. You are as common as muck." Sebastian gestured with a hand. "Immortality aside, obviously."

"Thanks," Isabelle said wryly.

"Do you mean to say that this—divine energy chooses who it bestows its power onto?" Elton said with a frown.

Sebastian shrugged. "Seeing as this is the first time I

am witnessing the phenomenon, I cannot state that for certain, but yes, it appears to select those whom it deems, well, worthy." He paused. "But I believe it is more than that." He gazed at Serena and Nate. "There is a bond between all of you who live here. And it is because of that bond that you two now share some of the divine essence possessed by the others."

Serena exchanged another bewildered look with Nate.

Artemus finally stirred, the surprise on his face replaced by curiosity. "I've been meaning to ask you. That thing Cunningham made. The cloud that choked us. What was it?"

"That I do not know." A troubled look washed across Sebastian's face. "He did not use it the first time I met him."

"By the way, how come you knew they were going to attack Artemus's shop?" Haruki frowned faintly at Serena. "You never did explain."

The Yakuza heir had been halfway to L.A. when Serena had called him that morning. Callie had messaged her en route to San Francisco to tell her she, Haruki, and Drake would be away for a couple of days. Serena had grown alarmed when she'd found that out. She'd told the three of them that Artemus was likely in grave danger and to return to Chicago immediately.

"Nate had been keeping track of Cunningham and his guards for the last few days. From the conversation Cunningham had with Artemus at the party, I knew he would likely try and make contact with him at his shop in Old Town."

Artemus narrowed his eyes. "So, you used us as bait?"

Serena clenched her fists. "I thought I would make it back in time."

Although she knew Artemus did not personally hold her or Sebastian responsible for the disappearance of his assistant, Otis's abduction weighed heavily on Serena's mind. She'd been confident that Artemus would be able to defend himself if anything were to happen to him in their absence. She hadn't banked on Otis getting caught in the crossfire.

"The device you used to incapacitate the super soldiers with Cunningham," Artemus said. "What was it?"

Serena looked at Nate and dipped her chin slightly. The super soldier removed a metal ball from his pocket and laid it on the table. Artemus and the others stared at it.

Lines furrowed Isabelle's brow. "Is that what I think it is?"

"Yeah," Serena muttered. "It's an EMP bomb. It's the one thing capable of disabling the nanorobots inside us, albeit temporarily."

Artemus picked up the device and studied it curiously.

"How come you and Nate weren't affected by it?" Drake asked.

"Our combat suits are coated with a Faraday shield. Gideon modified them when he realized we might have to go up against the first-generation super soldiers. He made new masks to protect our heads and gave them to me along with the EMP device."

Unease darkened Isabelle's eyes at that.

"This the same Gideon you spoke to that night, at the party?" Drake said.

Serena avoided his eyes. "Yes. He's the one I went to visit in Mexico."

"Incidentally, my bosses would very much like to know what you did with the bodies of the super soldiers

Artemus and Smokey killed." Isabelle's expression had grown cool. "They weren't there when Mark went to the shop fifteen minutes ago."

"Oh. Really?" Serena said innocently. "How very odd."

"Those bodies are the property of the Immortal Societies," Isabelle said icily.

Serena scowled. She rose to her feet and flattened her hands on the table. "Newsflash, blondie. *We* are not the property of anybody, understood?"

Elton straightened where he leaned against the counter and raised his hands in a pacifying gesture. "Now, now, ladies."

"I'm no lady!" Isabelle snapped at him.

"Neither am I!" Serena snarled.

"I would stay out of the angry Immortal and super soldier chick's way if I were you," Haruki told Elton.

"Cunningham also had nanorobots inside his body," Sebastian said quietly.

A frozen silence filled the room at his words.

"What?" Artemus mumbled.

Sebastian rubbed the back of his head. "I suppose you did not get to see it. It took the form of a weapon. A whip made of nanorobots that sprouted from his very arm. It acted as if it were alive. And, whatever I did to destroy it, the blasted thing just kept growing back."

Something that felt a lot like fear wormed its way inside Serena's heart then.

"So, not only has Ba'al somehow managed to merge demons with super soldiers, they've also incorporated our technology inside their human hosts?" she said grimly.

"It was the same with those super soldiers," Artemus added, troubled. "Their limbs can grow back too."

The color had drained from Isabelle's face. She

exchanged a shocked stare with Serena, all animosity forgotten. "That's end-of-the-world kinda bad right there."

"There's something else." Artemus drummed his fingers on the table. "The book that Cunningham brought for me to examine. It was a tome of poetry covered in black leather, with a red clasp. He said a colleague of his discovered it in Croatia. He wanted me to tell him its true origin. I can't help but feel that it's important to Ba'al." A muscle jumped in his cheek. "And I suspect his story was a lie."

Sebastian stiffened. "He brought a poetry book? From Croatia?"

"Yes." Artemus frowned. "Why?"

Sebastian faltered.

"Forgive me," he finally mumbled. "It is nothing."

Serena stared. It was evident the man was not being entirely truthful.

"Do you think Cunningham knew who you really were when he approached you?" Elton asked Artemus stiffly.

Artemus stopped drumming his fingers. "I believe so." His frown deepened. "He was evidently willing to take the risk of his identity being uncovered. Which means that book of poetry must be truly valuable."

"Why did Cunningham take Otis?" Callie said in the ensuing hush.

Sebastian's expression grew even more perturbed. "He saw one of Catherine Boone's journals. It was open on the floor."

Artemus's face fell. "Wait. Do you mean he—?"

Sebastian nodded. "Yes. I think he realized what it was from the few lines he read."

Lines wrinkled Drake's brow. "So, they want Otis

because they think he can tell them about the upcoming Judgement Day?"

"I believe that might be the case, yes," Sebastian replied, his face bleak.

Artemus fisted his hands. "But he can't."

"I know." Sebastian clenched his jaw. "I fear what they will do to him once they find that out."

"You're forgetting something," Callie said.

Artemus gazed at her, clearly upset. "What?"

"Otis is powerful, in his own mysterious way," Callie explained.

"She's right," Haruki murmured.

Artemus did not look vaguely reassured by their statements. "He doesn't know how to fight demons."

"What's our next move?" Drake's face hardened. "If Ba'al has Otis, shouldn't we be going after them?"

"We don't know where Cunningham's taken him," Serena said in a frustrated voice. "They could be anywhere in the world right now."

A sense of renewed urgency resonated around the kitchen.

"I'll contact the Vatican," Elton said. "See if they've seen any increase in demonic activity—"

"He is in England," Sebastian said flatly.

They stared at him.

"Trust me on this."

CHAPTER TWENTY-ONE

OTIS WOKE UP WITH A START. HE STARED AT THE shadowy ceiling above him before sitting up and looking around, his heart thumping erratically in his chest.

It took a few seconds for his eyes to adjust to the gloom. He was lying on a narrow bed, in a windowless room. There was a metal door set in the wall opposite him. Bar a small desk and a chair to his left, the chamber was empty.

The memory of what had happened back at the antique shop flashed before his eyes. Panic gripped him. He bolted from the bed on shaky legs and went over to the bureau. His fingers trembled as he frantically opened the drawers. They were empty. He knelt to look under the bed. There was nothing there.

Otis searched the room desperately with his gaze.

The bundle of journals he'd grabbed from the coffee table when Sebastian and the demon had stormed inside his apartment were nowhere to be seen.

A sudden chill raised goosebumps on his skin. Otis rubbed his arms briskly and stood frozen for a moment in the middle of the room, the fear twisting through his body so thick he thought he would choke on it.

He had no weapons with which to defend himself. Even if he had, he did not know how to fight demons. His knees almost buckled under the weight of the terror threatening to drown him.

He was going to die. He knew this as clearly as he knew he would be powerless to land a single blow on whichever fiendish creature tore into him first.

Footsteps sounded outside the room, startling him.

Otis backed away until his knees hit the bed.

The door opened. A man with long, white hair and an eyepatch walked into the room. A faded scar radiated outward on either side of the leather pad over his left eye. He stopped when he saw Otis. A pleasant smile curved his lips.

"Ah. You are awake at last."

Otis's pulse raced erratically. He was not fooled by the creature's benign look. This was the demon who had kidnapped him. He could tell from the cicatrix on the stranger's face and the odd smell that surrounded him.

"My name is Jacob Cunningham. I believe you are Otis Boone, Artemus Steele's assistant, correct?"

Otis swallowed and remained silent.

The smile faded from Cunningham's face. He sighed. "If you have no use for your tongue, I can ask one of my underlings to rip it out for you."

Shadows trembled in the corners of the room flanking the door. A whimper left Otis as two demons stepped out of the writhing darkness, their pupils glowing a sickening yellow.

"Of course, that would make translating the journals difficult," Cunningham said in a conversational tone. "But

I suppose you would still be able to write out the words at least."

Bile rose in Otis's throat. He stumbled to the nearest wall and heaved.

Cunningham and the demons watched silently while he threw up the meager contents of his stomach. Otis straightened shakily and wiped his mouth with the back of his hand, the bitter taste of acid coating his tongue.

"Oh dear," Cunningham drawled. "I do apologize. I did not think you would take my teasing so seriously."

He moved toward Otis.

"Stay away," Otis mumbled. He stepped back. "Don't come near me!"

Cunningham paused, his tone contrite. "Come now. I only wish for you to accompany me. Let us go to my study. I shall have someone serve us tea."

Otis faltered. He knew he had no choice but to obey the demon.

Cunningham guided him out of the room and into a corridor dotted with flaming torches sitting in metal brackets on the walls. Other doors appeared on either side of the passage in the flickering, yellow light.

Otis had the impression of being deep underground.

They negotiated several turns before coming to a stone staircase that spiraled upward. The two demons trailed in their wake as they ascended it, their talons clicking faintly against the rock while their ghastly shadows danced across the limestone walls.

Otis lost count of how many steps there were after a hundred. By the time they reached the top, he was sweating and out of breath. Being a shop assistant did not exactly require much in terms of stamina and the last time he'd worn gym clothes was when he was still in high school.

Cunningham appeared amused by his evident fatigue. "You are very different from your friends, aren't you?"

Otis swallowed, thinking of how Artemus and the others had battled the demons in Salem.

You can't even begin to understand how unalike we are!

The paralyzing fear that had taken hold of him was slowly abating. It didn't look like the demons were about to tear him to shreds just yet. Still, he knew he would be a fool if he were to let his guard down for even a moment.

Otis followed Cunningham as the man led the way through the building they now found themselves in, his curious gaze skimming the passages and rooms they passed. The chambers were deserted, their windows barred with wooden shutters and whatever bare furnishings they contained covered with dust sheets. The only ambient light he saw came from narrow, slit-like openings in the walls. All he could tell was that it was night outside; they were walking too fast for him to make out details of their location.

They came out into an enclosed yard, the transition from the inside to the outside so sudden it took Otis a moment to realize he was walking under a starlit sky. His eyes widened when he got his first look at the exterior of his prison.

"Is this a—a castle?!"

Cunningham did not reply. They entered another building.

This one looked lived in and was opulently furnished. It was also full of demons.

Some were in their human forms, the only hint of the monsters inside them the sinister, sulfurous light that lit up their pupils when they glanced curiously at Otis from where they lounged in low-lit rooms. Others were in their full fiendish manifestations and came in all shapes and sizes, their grotesque figures huddled in darkened corners and suspended from rafters.

Otis's stomach roiled when he saw some feasting on chunks of raw meat, blood dripping down their chins and coating their talons.

"Those are not human remains," Cunningham said lightly at Otis's expression.

This did little to reassure Otis.

They finally reached Cunningham's study. To Otis's surprise, the chamber was enormous and lined from floor to ceiling with books. An ornate metal staircase rose to the left and spiraled to an upper gallery that framed three walls.

Cunningham strolled toward a set of highback chairs arranged in front of a stone hearth at the head of the room, where a fire crackled. Otis's eyes widened when he saw his mother's journals stacked neatly on the coffee table in the middle of the seating area, next to a slim book with a black leather cover and a red clasp. He resisted the urge to rush over and grab his mother's legacy, conscious of the demonic escort who'd taken up guard position near the entrance.

Cunningham indicated one of the chairs with a faint smile. "Come, sit."

CHAPTER TWENTY-TWO

OTIS HESITATED BEFORE COMPLYING. CUNNINGHAM took the seat opposite him.

A man came in with a tray bearing a porcelain tea set, biscuits, and slices of cake, his demon eyes flickering briefly to Otis. Otis stared at the pretty China and the neatly arranged confectionary. He swallowed the manic laughter suddenly rising inside him.

This was without a doubt the most surreal experience he'd ever had. For a moment, he wondered if he was dead and this was the afterlife he was doomed to. He sobered at that thought.

Cunningham dismissed the demon and poured Otis a cup of tea.

Otis's stomach rumbled. Heat flooded his face at the monster's amused look.

"Please, help yourself to some cake."

This time, Otis obeyed eagerly. He wolfed down two slices without pausing for breath and finally felt his hunger abate. The tea was sweet and strong.

"How long have you been in Mr. Steele's employ?"

Otis tensed slightly at Cunningham's question. "Two years."

"And before that?" Cunningham murmured, settling back comfortably in his chair.

Otis hesitated. "I was at college."

Cunningham arched an eyebrow. "And you majored in?"

"Linguistics," Otis admitted reluctantly.

He regretted his confession straight away when he saw the shrewd light that flashed in the demon's eyes.

It wasn't until they had finished their drinks that Cunningham finally addressed the subject of his mother's journals.

"I believe you and Sebastian were studying these." The demon reached over and picked up one of the diaries. He leafed carelessly through it. "What can you tell me about them?"

"I—" Otis stopped and swallowed, his pulse racing with fear once more. "We found them dumped outside the shop one day, several months ago."

There was no way he was going to tell this man about his mother's visions or where they had actually discovered the journals.

"And you have been translating them?"

"Not successfully," Otis admitted reluctantly. "That's why Sebastian was helping us."

Cunningham smiled thinly. Otis knew the demon had seen through his lies.

"From the papers I glimpsed in that room where you were holed up, you seem to have made significant headway. Tell me, boy, what do these journals say?"

Otis remained quiet, his heart now beating so ferociously against his ribs he wondered if the demons could hear it.

"Do they mention a Judgement Day?" Cunningham continued insistently, his pupils flaring with a repugnant, yellow glow and his voice deepening into a growl. "Do they talk of the Gates of Hell and the beasts who hold the keys to opening them? Do they mention their locations?"

Otis shrank back in his seat, his stomach churning. He felt like throwing up again.

Cunningham's face hardened at his silence. "You refuse to speak?"

Otis felt the blood drain from his face as Cunningham rose, his figure shifting into that of the monster who dwelled within him, his gargantuan shadow engulfing Otis as his body swelled.

"Should I rip your tongue from your mouth?" the demon spat, flecks of drool staining his chin, his true nature manifesting itself at last. "Or gouge your eyes from your head?!"

Cunningham stormed across to where he sat, grabbed him by the front of his shirt, and hauled him to his feet. Otis recoiled as the demon thrust his face down into his, the creature's foul stench intensifying around them.

"You will tell me what is in those journals or I will tear you apart and feast on your organs while you watch, you insolent rat!" Cunningham roared.

The voice came like a whisper on a breeze, its sweet tone achingly familiar as it drifted through Otis's mind.

No.

Otis's eyes widened. *Mom?!*

"Talk, damn you!"

Cunningham raised his other hand and made to strike Otis.

Never.

"Never," Otis breathed.

Heat bloomed inside his chest. The air trembled around him.

Cunningham hissed and released him before clutching his hand, surprise widening his obsidian eyes for an instant. They both stared at the red marks on his flesh.

The room started to shake. The chandeliers creaked ominously above them as they swayed, caught in an invisible wind. Otis gazed from the China rattling on the coffee table to the books falling from the shelves on the walls.

Wait! Is that me?!

Blood pounded in his ears as he recalled the incident at his family farm, when his father first told them what his mother's journals contained, and the most recent experience at his apartment, on the day he told Haruki the name of his weapon.

Cunningham took a step toward him, his gaze dark with fury, the demon guards now at his side.

Otis put his hands up defensively.

The demons never reached him.

An explosive force wrapped around the three creatures and cast them across the room. They crashed into one of the bookcases, sending dozens of tomes thudding to the ground.

Otis was moving before he was even aware of it, his legs taking him to the door and into the corridor beyond at a dead run. His feet pounded the stone floor as he retraced his steps; he had memorized the layout of the passages they had navigated earlier, in case an opportunity to escape ever presented itself, however slim that chance was.

Shadows deepened around him as the demons in the castle gave chase, the creatures obeying their master's silent order. Though they tried to attack him, none managed to land a blow.

Otis knew that the heat flowing through his veins and vibrating through his bones was a power of some sort. A power that was keeping the creatures at bay. A power that could help him break free from his prison.

He found himself in the courtyard he and Cunningham had traversed earlier and bolted toward the steps he had spied, the demons' high-pitched screeches echoing in his wake. The staircase led to a wall-walk that ran along the length of a tall battlement.

Otis bolted down the passageway until he came to the roof of a round tower edged by a crenellated parapet. He grabbed the thick wall where a gap opened up and leaned out, hoping to find an escape route or someone he could shout to for help.

The sight that met his eyes had his stomach plummeting to his boots.

A dark, roiling sea stretched out into nothingness from the base of the towering cliffs upon which the keep stood. A spot of light broke dimly through the pitch blackness on the horizon before pulsing out of existence.

It took a moment for Otis to realize he was looking at a distant lighthouse across an expanse of ocean.

We're on an island!

A noise behind him had him twisting on his heels. Dread filled him when he saw the demons gathering around him.

"No!" Otis shouted, his voice trembling. "*Stay away from me!*"

The force radiating from his body intensified. The demons gnashed their teeth and howled in rage as an invisible wall of energy pushed their bodies back, their claws raising sparks on the stone floor.

A putrid miasma started to seep across the roof of the tower. Cunningham appeared through the crowd of fiends. Otis's eyes widened. The noxious vapor was exuding out of the demon's lips.

No!

Otis covered his mouth and nose with his hands and could only watch helplessly as the vile smoke finally reached him, his power useless in the face of something so insubstantial. The poison seeped through his skin and entered his blood. The heat faded from Otis's veins. His vision clouded over. He swayed and started to fall.

It was in that moment that a name came to him.

The name of the demon who possessed Cunningham.

CHAPTER TWENTY-THREE

Artemus gazed out of the SUV window. A light drizzle fell from the overcast sky, swamping the landscape on either side of the motorway in shades of gray.

England was damp, cold, and dreary. It was a different kind of cold to the constant winds that blasted Chicago. This cold soaked into his skin and the very marrow of his bones, as insidious as the poisonous vapor Cunningham had exuded back at the shop and sapping him of energy. Smokey looked as lethargic as he felt where he perched on Callie's lap.

Sebastian, on the other hand, appeared bright and perky in the driver's seat.

Artemus frowned. Though Callie and Haruki had offered their private planes for their trip to England, Sebastian had proposed they use his instead.

"You have a jet?" Drake had asked skeptically when Sebastian first mentioned this.

"I do," Sebastian had admitted.

Two SUVs had been waiting for them on the tarmac of the small, private airfield where they'd landed in England that afternoon. To everyone's surprise, the airfield director had been there to meet them and had practically kowtowed to Sebastian when he'd stepped off the plane. It had taken a moment for Artemus to notice that the golden lion symbol on Sebastian's plane was reflected on the side of the airfield's hangars.

Judging from what he'd seen thus far, it was clear to Artemus that Sebastian had been less than generous with the truth when it came to how he made a living. The guy was evidently as rich as Croesus.

"Bookstore owner my ass," Drake muttered darkly where he sat next to Sebastian.

Sebastian arched an eyebrow. "What do you mean?"

Their convoy was travelling briskly along a highway, Haruki, Serena, and Nate following in the second SUV behind them. They were on their way to Oxford, where Cunningham lived and worked. When asked why he seemed so convinced the demon had returned to England, Sebastian had said, "Demons always go back home."

"What, like Lassie?" Artemus had asked incredulously.

They had all stared at him blankly.

"It's an old movie, about a dog who makes his way back to his master after he's sold off to someone else," Artemus had explained, his tone turning defensive.

"You're showing your age," Serena had said wryly.

They came off the highway a short while later and entered the outskirts of the city. The distant spires of churches and the iconic buildings of Oxford University appeared against the darkening sky as they crossed a bridge, the structures almost eldritch in the gathering dusk. They convened in a store car park before splitting up into two groups, Sebastian, Artemus, Smokey, and Serena taking one of the SUVs while Drake, Nate, Callie, and Haruki took the other.

"Looks like you know this place well," Serena observed as Sebastian drove expertly through the city's one-way system.

"I should do." Sebastian glanced at her. "I was a student here for many years." He paused. "That *was* over a century ago but the roads are still the same."

Artemus pondered this as they slowed at a traffic light. It was becoming clear that there was still a lot they didn't know about Sebastian.

Night had fallen by the time they pulled up outside a sprawling Victorian mansion in a leafy suburb to the north of the city. Artemus eyed the few lit windows peppering the building's facade warily.

It was the theology college where Cunningham apparently held office. Though they knew the chances of finding the demon and Artemus's missing assistant there were unlikely, they hoped to at least find a clue to their potential whereabouts.

"So, what's our game plan?" Artemus said when they stepped out of the SUV. "Do we just walk in there?"

"Of course not," Sebastian said contemptuously.

Serena cast a pitiful look at Artemus. "We break in."

"It worries me how blasé you two are about engaging in criminal activity on foreign soil," Artemus said dully.

Smokey huffed in agreement next to him.

"I was born in this country," Sebastian retorted gruffly. "Besides which, this is my alma mater."

They found a junction box at the end of the street. Serena connected her laptop to it while Sebastian, Artemus, and Smokey kept a lookout.

"You seem very experienced with this kind of undertaking," Sebastian declared as he watched her fingers fly over her laptop keyboard.

"Yeah, well, this is a walk in the park for a mercenary," Serena murmured, her eyes on the screen.

A horrified expression dawned on Sebastian's face. "You are a soldier of fortune?!"

"Will you pipe down?" Serena glanced around the dark street. "You're making a ruckus."

"I did not know this," Sebastian mumbled to Artemus.

"What, that she and Nate are guns for hire?" Artemus said drily. "You should ask Drake how they met. Incidentally, I'm still convinced you're not telling us everything you know either."

Sebastian evaded his shrewd gaze.

"I'm in the building's security system," Serena said a moment later. "Cunningham's office is on the second floor, in the left wing. I'm locking down their camera network for one hour." She paused. "There are twenty people in there according to the heat signatures on the satellite infrared cam. Most of them are in the right wing. I guess that's where the student accommodations are."

Artemus grimaced. He should have known she'd hacked into one of the Immortals' satellite networks. From a conversation he'd overheard between her and Nate a month ago, it was something the super soldiers did regularly. It was an act of rebellion against their former masters.

"Twenty people doesn't seem like a lot."

"It's summer break," Sebastian said.

Artemus shivered and hunched his shoulders against the cold. "*This* is summer?"

They ended up forcing open the window of a utility room at the rear of the building. A corridor led them past a communal staff room and admin offices. The sound of a TV traveled faintly down a hall to their left when they reached the backstairs. They headed silently to the second floor.

Cunningham's office was at the end of a passage that overlooked the side gardens. Serena closed the door after them and switched the overhead light on. Artemus looked around curiously.

The room was surprisingly normal. A coat stand stood to the right of the door. On the opposite side of the chamber, beyond a Persian rug with frayed edges that covered old, polished floorboards, an antique desk and leather chairs occupied the space in front of a bay window. All around them were cases and cabinets stacked with books.

Serena walked across to a bookcase and ran her fingers lightly over the spine of a bible. "Is it just me or does anyone else find it creepy that a demon is a theology professor at one of the most reputable universities in the world?"

Artemus grimaced. "It's not just you."

They spent the next fifteen minutes searching the room. To Artemus's annoyance, they found nothing that suggested Cunningham's current location.

"Now what?" Serena said.

She stood in the middle of the room, her hands on her hips and a frown clouding her face.

Artemus let out a frustrated sigh. "We meet up with the others and see if they found any clues at the second location, I guess."

A muscle twitched in Sebastian's jawline. "I hate to admit it, but I fear you are correct."

They headed for the exit.

Artemus paused when they reached the door. "Smokey?"

The rabbit was standing in front of a bookcase to their right. He was staring intently at the middle shelf.

Can you smell that?

Artemus and Sebastian glanced at each other in surprise.

"Smell what?"

Artemus crossed the floor to the rabbit, Sebastian in his wake.

Serena followed. "What is it? Did Smokey sniff something out?"

"Is it Cunningham's scent?" Sebastian asked stiffly.

Yes. It is the same odor I smelled at the shop. It is strongest here.

"We've already examined the contents of those shelves," Artemus said, puzzled.

There is something behind those books.

Artemus and Sebastian grabbed the ends of the case and dragged it forward.

It was Serena who found the symbol. They stared at the inverted pentagram painted in faint, black lines on the dark wallpaper.

"Wait," she murmured, "isn't that—?"

"The Sigil of Baphomet," Sebastian concluded in a grim voice.

Artemus frowned. It was the same symbol they'd discovered in L.A., during the demon uprising that had preceded the murder of Haruki's brother.

CHAPTER TWENTY-FOUR

"How can a university professor afford a place like this?" Drake muttered.

They stared at the dark residence looming against the night sky ahead of them.

Cunningham's house was at the end of a cul-de-sac, one-and-a-half mile north of the city. It had extensive grounds and a lawned garden that ended in a jetty opening onto a river.

"Academics are paid really well," Nate stated laconically.

Haruki shivered. "This place gives me the creeps."

Callie sighed and looked at her boots. They had had to cross a field to approach the property from the rear and her new shoes were covered in mud.

"I could have carried you," Nate said when he saw her grimace.

Callie narrowed her eyes at him. "No, thanks. I can walk just fine."

Drake and Haruki exchanged a glance at her curt tone. It was evident that Callie had had something on her mind all day. And that something appeared to be the hulking super soldier who was currently gazing at her impassively.

"Let's get on with this."

Callie gripped her cane and stormed across the lawn.

"Hey, wait a minute!" Drake hissed. "We don't know if there are—"

"She's not listening to you," Haruki said.

Drake blew out an exasperated sigh. They headed after her.

Callie was waiting for them on a side terrace. "I don't think there's anyone home."

She cupped her hands around her face and pressed her nose against a wide French door.

Drake had to reluctantly agree. If there had been demons about, he would have felt it by now. He frowned faintly.

Of course, Cunningham isn't just a regular demon. I didn't sense anything from him at Elton's party. Which means he must be a demon commander, like Daniel Delacourt and Erik Park.

It was Delacourt who had revealed to Callie that the most powerful demons could mask their auras, when he'd first confronted her and Smokey in L.A.

Drake picked the lock on the back door. A heavy silence greeted them when they entered the house.

Haruki rubbed his arms against the chill. "Like I said, spooky."

They spent half an hour exploring the first floor and found nothing of interest. It was when they were headed up to the second floor that Callie suddenly stopped, turned, and frowned at Nate where he'd paused on the steps below her.

"If we're going to do this, I expect to be wooed," she

declared, pointing a commanding finger at the super soldier.

Drake stared. "Really? You want to do this here? *Now?*"

"Hold on," Haruki hissed. "Things are getting interesting!"

Callie ignored them and arched an eyebrow at the super soldier. "Well?"

Nate blinked, as if coming out of a daze. "Okay."

"I expect flowers, chocolate, wining and dining, the lot," Callie stated adamantly.

Drake leaned toward Haruki. "Can he afford to wine and dine her? She's used to some expensive places."

Haruki hushed him.

"And no sex before the third date," Callie added, her cheeks pinking slightly.

Nate hesitated. "Does this mean you want to go out with me?"

Callie scowled. "Of course it does, you buffoon! And you are allowed to carry me, but only under special circumstances!"

She twisted on her heels and flounced up the stairs.

Drake put a hand on Nate's shoulder. "Good luck. You're gonna need it."

"Ogawa told me about these herbs for sexual stamina," Haruki added. "Let me know if you want some."

"I believe I am more than adequate in that department," Nate murmured.

"You guys know I can hear you, right?!" Callie snapped from the top of the steps.

～

"YOU KNOW WHAT WE COULD DO WITH RIGHT NOW?" Serena said.

"What?" Sebastian murmured.

"One of your magic balls. It'd be stronger than this torch." Something skittered across the ground in front of them in the faint glow of her pen light. "And I bet it'd keep the rats away too."

Artemus nodded. "She's right. Light the way, shiny fingers."

Sebastian cast him a dirty look.

Smokey's eyes glittered red ahead of them as he looked over his shoulder, his hellhound shape invisible in the darkness.

This way.

They were in an underground tunnel somewhere south of the theology college. The wall featuring the Sigil of Baphomet had masked a hidden door that revealed a cramped staircase built into the very walls of the Victorian mansion. Smokey had melted the lock on the metal door at the bottom of the stairs with a trickle of pee and tracked Cunningham's scent through the passages they'd found beyond.

They turned a corner presently and reached a junction. Smokey stopped, his ears cocking backward and forward as he scrutinized the tunnels on either side of them.

Artemus tensed at the vibe resonating from the hellhound across the bond that connected them. "What is it?"

There are other demon scents down here. They are coming from both directions.

"What's the pooch saying?" Serena asked.

Artemus frowned. "We may have company."

He took out his switchblade.

Serena removed a dagger from one of the sheaths on her thighs.

Sebastian reached for the pocket watch in his vest. The antique piece transformed smoothly in his grip, the golden lash moving through the air as if it were sentient.

Smokey eyed the whip warily before heading right.

The odor of the demon Cunningham is strongest in this passage.

The air grew colder the farther along the tunnel they advanced. The darkness thickened ahead. Artemus blinked when a spark of light suddenly flared into existence in Sebastian's right hand.

Sebastian traced a faint mark on the wall to the right with his fingers. "I think I know where we are."

"We're under the Bodleian Library," Serena said.

Sebastian looked at her suspiciously. "How do you know that?"

Serena pointed at her smartband. "This thing has GPS."

"Oh." Sebastian sniffed. "Well, this place is part of an underground tunnel system that was built in the early twentieth century to store books. As far as the public knows, these passages go from the Bodleian to Radcliffe Square."

Artemus and Serena exchanged a glance.

"What do you mean, as far as the public knows?" Artemus said.

"It means there was more than one tunnel system constructed at the time."

They came to a set of abandoned rail tracks and ventured deeper inside the maze of burrows. Smokey slowed a moment later, a low growl rumbling from his throat.

Artemus clenched his fingers, sent a burst of power to the knife in his hand, and reached for the gun at his back. The blade transformed into a pale longsword.

He could feel the demons' presence now.

It was Sebastian who found the second Sigil of Baphomet carved into a limestone brick. He depressed it, his knuckles whitening on the weapon in his hand. A low groan echoed around the tunnel as a section of wall retracted by several feet, revealing narrow steps twisting into darkness.

The first demon appeared when they were halfway down the staircase.

CHAPTER TWENTY-FIVE

"ARE YOU SURE THEY'RE HERE?" CALLIE SAID DUBIOUSLY.

"Yes. The GPS tracker on Serena's smartband is pinpointing her location to this place." Nate paused. "She's not answering my call though."

"Neither is Artemus." Drake tucked his cell back into his jeans and made a face. "That piece of junk he calls a phone probably doesn't have signal around here."

They gazed at the imposing tower dominating the facade of the historic building before them.

Cunningham's home had not yielded any clues as to his or Otis's whereabouts. They'd finally abandoned their search and decided to regroup with the others. Nate's directions had led them back into the very heart of the city and the university campus.

They earned some curious stares from passers-by as they stood indecisively before the Bodleian Library.

Callie tensed. "Are you guys sensing that?"

"Sensing what?" Nate said.

Callie glanced worriedly at Haruki and Drake. "Demons."

Drake clenched his jaw and nodded. He could tell from the way the monster inside him was stirring that some of his fiendish brethren were close by.

"They're underground," Haruki said in a hard voice.

He was staring at a metal grate on the street. Steam swirled faintly from the holes at its edges.

They found another access point free from inquisitive eyes in a side alley that branched off a square next to the library. The sewers beneath were surprisingly cool and dry.

Nate removed a pen light from his pocket and looked at his smartband. "This way."

The demonic energy grew stronger the farther they pressed on. Drake gritted his teeth as his devil's powers surged, talons scraping insidiously against the prison that bound him, his sibilant voice urging Drake to surrender to his dark nature.

Soon, they were inside a complex system of tunnels. They had just turned a corner when Nate stopped abruptly.

"What's wrong?" Callie said.

Nate's face hardened. "Serena. Her signal just disappeared."

"We don't need the GPS," Haruki said, his voice lowering to a growl.

Smoke curled from his nostrils and mouth. His pupils shifted into orange, vertical slits. The juzu bracelet on his right wrist trembled, the eyes of the dragon on the main bead glowing red before the entire thing transformed into a pale, flaming sword. Silver scales sprouted on his hands and face.

Callie transformed into her beast form beside him, her cane glimmering silver and gold as it changed into the deadly Scepter of Gabriel, her hair a mass of writhing, flaxen snakes around her face.

Drake unleashed his own blade and shield. "Haruki's right. We can practically taste the demons' trail."

They hurried through the warren of passages and soon came across a set of rail lines. A distant screech echoed toward them. They broke into a dead run.

Flashes of light flared faintly in the gloom ahead, outlining the edges of a concealed doorway. Booms and demonic screams echoed from the staircase beyond.

They found Artemus and the others in a large underground pit at the bottom.

SERENA GRUNTED AS SOMETHING LANDED ON HER BACK and pushed her hard against the cold, stone wall.

She clenched her teeth and heaved against the three demons piled atop her, their talons scoring her combat suit in vain. Metal crunched under her feet, the shards of her broken smartband glinting faintly in the gloom where it had come off her wrist.

One of the demons shrieked and tumbled off her. Serena glimpsed Smokey out the corner of her eye; the hellhound was tearing savagely into the fallen creature's throat where he had knocked him to the floor of the pit. She narrowed her eyes, dropped to one knee, and slashed backward with both her blades.

Hot wetness stained her hands where she carved into her attackers' flesh. The demons howled and stumbled backward. Serena flipped forward onto her hands and twisted, her legs scissoring through the air before wrapping around the neck of one of the demons and bringing him to the ground. A savage snarl left her as she drove her elbow into his throat, snapping his windpipe and his spine. The creature shuddered violently for timeless seconds before growing still, his body shrinking into his human shape in death.

The other demon lunged toward her just as she jumped to her feet, his claws aimed at her eyes. He came to a sudden halt inches from her. A comical expression of shock dawned on his face. His obsidian gaze dropped to the dark sword that had just impaled him from behind.

A grisly, wet sound came as Drake slowly withdrew the weapon. He slashed the demon from behind, almost severing his neck. The creature went limp, choked gurgles escaping him, black blood frothing at his lips. The light went out of his eyes as he collapsed to the ground.

Serena's pulse thumped rapidly as she glanced around the demon den. Callie, Haruki, and Nate had also joined the battle. Now that they were here, the demon horde they'd stumbled upon was being rapidly decimated.

She gazed into Drake's red pupils. "How did you—?"

"Nate tracked your smartband signal until a short while ago. We could sense the demons' energy after that."

The air tore above them with a deafening noise. A rift appeared some thirty feet above their heads, its edges glowing crimson.

Serena frowned at the demons coming out of the portal. "I really hate those winged bastards."

∾

SEBASTIAN STARED AT THE CREATURES SWARMING OUT OF the breach in space. "What in the devil are those?!"

"You've not seen these guys before?" Artemus said before shooting a demon in the chest.

The creature gasped. His eyes widened as fiery lines flared from the gaping wound in his ribcage. He screamed and burst into flames.

"No, I have not."

Sebastian waved at the cloud of ash tumbling past his face before casting a lightning ball distractedly at the two demons charging toward them from one of the tunnels that branched off the main chamber.

The creatures fell, their bodies burning and crumbling to dust.

"Hey, watch it, sunshine!" Callie snapped behind them. "That one almost caught me!"

The golden snakes framing her face hissed angrily at Sebastian. She drew her arm back and cast her scepter, impaling two winged demons like meat on a stick.

"Sorry," Sebastian mumbled.

He studied Callie curiously. It was his first time witnessing his sister's Chimera form.

She is very skillful.

Motion above drew his gaze. Four of the winged demons were diving toward where he and Artemus stood near the east wall of the pit. Sebastian drew on his power and prepared to crack his golden whip, his beast glaring fiercely at the fiends from behind his eyes.

Oh.

Sebastian blinked at his beast's surprised interjection. It was a couple of seconds before he sensed what the creature had just felt.

Artemus's power was surging rapidly beside him.

"Guess I'm gonna need my wings for this," the antique shop owner muttered.

Blinding light filled the room, the explosion of energy so strong it thumped painfully against Sebastian's eardrums. He blinked and raised a hand protectively to shield his eyes. His vision slowly cleared. He drew a sharp breath at what he saw.

White wings framed Artemus's silhouette as he rose into the air, his figure covered by golden armor and his skin the color of molten silver where it was exposed beneath it. The blade in his hand was now a broadsword as tall as him and edged with pale flames.

Drake ascended on the opposite side of the room, his wings the same color as the black armor that shielded his frame, his eyes red and gold. Fire bloomed on his fingertips where his right hand wrapped around the handle of his serrated broadsword. On his left arm was an enormous shield, the metal dulled a dark gray except where it glowed with crimson runes.

The angels moved. The demons screamed.

It was only thanks to his beast that Sebastian managed to somehow follow Artemus and Drake's lightning-fast attacks above them. Unease filtered through him at the wicked energy pulsing from Drake. In that moment, the man's life force was almost indistinguishable from that of a demon.

Some of the creatures managed to retreat into the rift. The ones who were too slow fell beneath the ruthless blades of the angels who flanked them, their attackers' strikes synchronized to perfection, as if they were one being instead of two.

The portal closed with a thunderous clap a moment later.

Artemus and Drake came down, their feet touching

the ground soundlessly as they landed, their weapons shrinking in their hands. They transformed back into their human shapes.

Artemus gazed morosely around the chamber. All that remained of the demons were piles of ash and dust.

"Well, there goes our chance of finding a clue to Cunningham's whereabouts." He turned to Drake. "Any joy at his house?"

"No."

Serena grimaced. "We should have tried to keep one of those demons alive."

"It's too late for that now," Haruki muttered.

Someone sneezed behind them. They turned.

Smokey shook his head to clear the ash from his muzzle and carried on rooting through the mound before him.

Sebastian frowned. "What is he doing?"

Smokey made a pleased huff. He plucked out something rectangular in his fangs and padded over to them. The object fluttered to the ground as he released it. Sebastian crouched down and picked it up.

"What is it?" Artemus said curiously.

Sebastian straightened and scrutinized the faded drawing on the thin cardboard. "It's the Tower. A Major Arcana tarot card." He flipped it over. There were three words written in crimson letters on the back. "The Drunken Minstrel."

Callie brightened. "A clue!"

"I suspect this is a drinking establishment," Sebastian said thoughtfully. "There are bound to be dozens by this name, though. Still, well done."

He patted Smokey's head.

The hellhound's eyes rounded. He looked sheepishly at Sebastian before licking his hand. The rest of them stared.

Sebastian blinked. "I am experiencing a warm, tingling feeling."

"That would be the acid drool," Artemus said.

CHAPTER TWENTY-SIX

"He has no marks on him?"

Cunningham crouched on one knee in front of the crimson portal, head bowed and gaze focused on the stone floor of the keep's main tower. "No, my liege."

The malevolent force of Ba'al's supreme leader washed over him in violent waves that made his very bones tremble, the pressure of his presence so great Cunningham knew it would have crushed his human form were he not possessed by a strong demon.

Low level demons could not tolerate being close to Ba'al's leader for any length of time, even through the medium of a rift. Cunningham had too often witnessed how it rendered them insane, some even going as far as to gouge their eyes out and rip their own bodies to pieces.

"And you believe these journals he has may hold the key to revealing the information we have long sought?" his leader said, his voice a thunderous sound that made the air quake.

"Yes, my liege. Although they are but duplicates of the original records, the little I have seen of their content bears a strong resemblance to some of our own demonic scriptures."

Cunningham hesitated, wondering if he should admit to his one grave mistake.

"I must apologize," he finally murmured. "The items we have in our possession are but part of a larger collection. I was not in a position to obtain all of them during my battle with our enemies."

The corrupt energy pulsing from the portal intensified. Cracks appeared in the floor around Cunningham's feet. He clenched his jaw as his body was pushed farther into the ground.

"I do not tolerate failure!" Ba'al's leader hissed.

Cunningham waited breathlessly for the punishment he knew he deserved, his heart pounding in his chest. The wall of evil bearing down on him eased as their leader's rage abated.

"But I have known you for a long time. You are our brother, after all." His leader's tone turned meditative. "Remember this well. You are part of His trusted circle and one of the Princes of Hell. As such, your actions reflect upon us all. I approved your proposal to take the tome we had discovered to Artemus Steele. Make sure that I do not come to regret my decision."

The rift closed with a boom that reverberated in Cunningham's ears. Night fell around him once more. He waited a moment before rising to his feet, the encounter with Ba'al's supreme leader having left him slightly shaky, as it always did. A strong wind ruffled his hair and cooled his skin. He stared out over the ocean beyond the battlements, anger swirling through him.

I will not fail my brethren again.

Cunningham turned and headed back into the castle.

The demons he came across scattered in his path, no doubt sensing the fury boiling off him. He made his way down the long, winding staircase that led to the dungeons and strode inside Otis Boone's prison.

Artemus Steele's assistant raised his head from his knees where he sat huddled on the floor in a corner of the chamber, his face pale and his eyes dark with fear. Cunningham stormed toward him.

The barrier struck him seconds later, an invisible force that wrapped like a bubble around the figure cowering on the floor. Cunningham gnashed his teeth as the wall singed his skin. He stepped back.

The power protecting Otis Boone had remained even after he'd succumbed to Cunningham's miasma last night, following his escape attempt. It had been with some difficulty that they had managed to transport his unconscious body back to the dungeons, the demons assigned to the task growling and moaning in pain as the young man's life force scorched their flesh.

It was many hours before the prisoner awoke from his poison-induced slumber. Now that he was conscious again, the wall around him had strengthened to the point where he could keep demons from approaching him once more.

Cunningham scowled. Their man inside the Vatican had never said anything about Artemus Steele's assistant possessing powers that equaled those of his employer and his allies.

Is it because he never participated in the prior battles with Ba'al? Or have Steele and his cronies been hiding him from our eyes?

Whatever the answer was, Cunningham was certain of one thing. Otis Boone was the key to unravelling the prophecies contained in the journals he had been studying.

And maybe even decoding the sacred scrolls we have been unable to decipher to date.

His hands curled into fists. There was only one thing he could think of that could force Artemus Steele's assistant to cooperate with them.

"HOW FAR IS THIS PLACE?"

Sebastian glanced broodingly at Callie where she sat in the passenger seat next to him. "We're already on the grounds of the estate."

Her eyes widened. She stared out the window of the SUV. "We are?"

Smokey rose in her lap and placed his paws on the glass, his rabbit nose twitching curiously.

They were driving down a dark country lane lined with thick woodland. The only hint of approaching daybreak was a faint, red light in the sky beyond the tree line to the east.

"This is a private road," Sebastian murmured.

"Dude, just how rich are you?" Haruki said from the back seat.

Sebastian was aware of Artemus's gaze drilling into his nape. It distracted him somewhat from the melancholy building inside him as they approached his family's mansion.

Nearly two centuries had passed since he'd witnessed the gruesome aftermath of his family's brutal killing. Although he often came to England on business, it had been some years since he had returned home; he could only tolerate being in the place for so long before he was almost overwhelmed by the sorrow of their loss.

A pair of imposing, black, wrought-iron gates appeared in the SUV's headlights. The woodland extended beyond them, forming a living screen that shielded the estate from curious eyes. The mansion finally came into view after they crossed a stone bridge spanning a gurgling river, its pale, hulking shape looming above the landscaped gardens surrounding it. They drove up the graveled driveway and pulled into a forecourt flanked by the two wings of the manor.

The second SUV rolled to a stop behind them. Drake, Serena, and Nate alighted from the vehicle.

Drake studied the imposing limestone facade of the English country home. "How old is this place?"

"It was built in the early seventeenth century, although its foundations were laid much earlier than that," Sebastian replied reluctantly. "It was primarily a Jacobean house. Our ancestors added other architectural elements to it over the years."

Nate glanced at Serena, his expression strangely wistful. "It reminds me of our father's home."

"It's a long story," Serena explained at Sebastian's puzzled look. "And one that I have no intention of telling you guys."

The sun peeked above the horizon just as they entered the mansion. Sebastian stepped inside the echoey entrance hall and paused, the silence wrapping around him like a heavy mantle.

Dust motes danced in the bright rays coming through the tall, mullioned windows framing the main doors. The light struck the crystal chandeliers suspended from the richly plastered ceiling and cast a myriad of fragmented, colorful beams onto the antique furnishings around them and the massive, oak staircase rising up ahead.

At the top of the first flight of stairs, dominating the wall on the split-level landing, was a giant frame covered with a dust sheet. Memories flooded Sebastian as he stared at it.

Hidden behind the covering was the Lancaster family's last group portrait.

The artist, a renowned figure in the art world, had been commissioned from London and had visited the estate every week over a period of six months to paint the enormous, oil canvas. It had been a most amusing period in their lives, what with Sebastian barely able to keep still for his poses and his sisters constantly ribbing him for that fact while their parents looked on benevolently, the latter only intervening when the artist let out heavy sighs.

Sebastian swallowed past the sudden lump in his throat and turned away from the others. "There are plenty of bedrooms on the second floor of the west wing where you can rest. I'll be in the study if you need me."

He headed left down the hallway.

"What about the east wing?" Artemus asked curiously behind him.

Sebastian stiffened slightly and stopped in his tracks. "That wing is closed. I would prefer it if you did not wander there."

He was conscious of their stares on his back as he strolled along the corridor, his footsteps loud on the marble floor. A shuffling sound drew his gaze downward.

Smokey was hopping beside him, his bashful brown gaze looking everywhere but at Sebastian.

Sebastian sighed. "Come along then."

CHAPTER TWENTY-SEVEN

ARTEMUS'S CELL BUZZED, ROUSING HIM FROM A DEEP sleep. He rolled over and grabbed his phone from where it lay on the mattress next to him. Elton's number flashed on the screen. He sat up and took the call.

"Hey. What's up?"

"The Vatican just contacted me. There are rumors going around about a possible incident in Oxford involving demons," Elton said tersely. "Something about the Bodleian?"

Guilt flashed through Artemus. He grimaced and rubbed the back of his head. "Oh. You heard about that, huh?"

"Please tell me you didn't vandalize one of the most important historic libraries in the world," Elton said stiffly.

Artemus winced. "We didn't. All the action happened underground." He paused. "How did the Vatican find out anyway? It's not as if we blew up the place. And it only happened a few hours ago."

Elton hesitated. "From what I deduced from talking to

Isabelle, they have...people who sometimes assist them on these matters."

"People?" Artemus frowned and swung his legs over the side of the bed. "You mean, Immortals?"

Elton remained silent.

Artemus sighed. "Tell the Vatican there's a demon den in the tunnels close to the Bodleian Library. We found a secret door in Cunningham's office that led us to it. The place is a veritable maze. Sebastian thinks it's been there for a long time. We found a lot of old human remains in the secondary passages branching off the main lair."

"We heard of unexplained disappearances in and around Oxford at a meeting of the Vatican Group last year," Elton said after a short silence. "Our British branch was convinced demons were involved, but has never been able to prove it. They'll be pleased to know of this discovery."

"We can send them the exact coordinates if they want," Artemus said grudgingly.

"Thanks. More to the point, did you discover any leads to Otis and Cunningham's location?"

"Smokey sniffed something out when we were down there. It's a tarot card representing the Tower. There's the name of a tavern on the back." Artemus made a face. "Drake had a quick look on the internet. Sebastian was right. There are dozens of places by that name just in England alone."

"Do you think it's another demon lair?"

"Probably. Or a key meeting place of some sort. Anyway, I'll keep you updated with developments."

"Where are you, exactly?"

Artemus looked around the bedroom filled with period pieces and pretty furnishings. Though it was evident

Sebastian had not lived here for some time, the place was pristine, to the point he half expected to walk out of the door and see an aristocratic family and their Victorian servants wandering around the mansion. His gaze moved to the windows to his left and the peaceful, rolling countryside and woodland extending as far as the eye could see.

"We're at Sebastian's family home."

SEBASTIAN WOKE UP TO THE SMELL OF FRESHLY BREWED coffee and warm sunlight on his face. He looked around groggily.

Two steaming cups sat on the low table next to him. Artemus occupied one of the chairs on the other side, opposite the elegant divan where he lay. He was studying Sebastian thoughtfully, his elbows on his knees and his chin atop his interlinked fingers.

Sebastian made to rise.

"Don't," Artemus said quietly. "You'll wake him."

Sebastian stilled and looked down.

Smokey was sleeping on his chest, his weight a heavy, comforting warmth. A faint snore rumbled out of the rabbit's lips, making them tremble. His left hindleg kicked out feebly before settling back down on Sebastian's vest.

"Is he dreaming?"

"Yeah," Artemus murmured. "I doubt they're warm, fuzzy dreams though."

Sebastian relaxed back down on the couch. "Is watching people sleep a fetish of yours?"

Artemus ignored the wry question. "What are you not telling us?"

Sebastian's pulse jumped. He'd known this was coming

for some time and was surprised it had taken Artemus so long to dig deeper. He broke eye contact with the other man and gazed out of the study windows at the rear gardens and the low hedge maze that dominated its center. Beyond it, straddling a grassy knoll overlooking a small lake, was the orangery.

It had been his mother and his sisters' favorite place to spend an afternoon when they were still alive. Though Sebastian employed two local companies to service the house and maintain his lands, the greenhouse had remained empty since his family's murder.

"You're hiding something. And whatever that something is, I can't help but feel that it's important." Artemus faltered. "We've been through a lot in the short time that we've known each other. You know you can trust us." He made a frustrated sound and threw his hands up in the air. "You are Smokey and Callie's brother, for God's sake, so at least trust them, if you won't—"

"I know where my gate is."

Artemus froze at his words. His jaw dropped.

Smokey opened one eye and stared at Sebastian.

"*What?!*" Artemus blurted out.

Sebastian sat up and swung his legs over the edge of the divan. Smokey sprung from his chest to the table and turned to watch him, his chocolate gaze dark with surprise.

"I know where my gate is." Sebastian sighed. "Or half of it anyway."

The study door opened with a sudden clatter. Callie, Haruki, Drake, Serena, and Nate fell inside the room atop one another in a loud, noisy pile.

"I told you two not to push," Nate mumbled where he lay at the bottom.

"Sorry," Haruki said guiltily.

"Yeah," Drake muttered.

Serena gave the pair a dirty look as they climbed off her.

Artemus narrowed his eyes at them. "Eavesdropping? *Really?*"

Callie scrambled to her feet and dusted her hands. "You were taking too long."

"She was worried you guys might get into an argument," Serena said.

"What, like five-year-olds in a sandpit?" Artemus snapped.

"You blew your top when Nate rearranged the cutlery drawer when we first moved in," Serena stated flatly.

"You ranted at me for a whole ten minutes when I parked my bike close to the porch two months ago," Drake added.

"Never mind what you did to poor Haruki when he broke that Qing Dynasty vase," Callie muttered.

Haruki shuddered. "Don't remind me."

"I thought we promised never to talk about the Qing Dynasty vase incident," Artemus said grimly.

"Sorry," Callie mumbled. She turned to Sebastian, concern clouding her eyes. "What's this about a gate?"

CHAPTER TWENTY-EIGHT

SEBASTIAN'S EXPRESSION GREW STRAINED.

"We're not leaving this room until you tell us more, so you might as well get comfortable, pal," Artemus said coolly.

Sebastian picked up his cup of coffee and drank a sip distractedly. He went still and stared into his drink. Lines furrowed his brow.

"Wait. Did you go shopping? I am pretty sure the last time I checked my larder, it was empty."

"We went into the nearby village while you guys were sleeping," Serena said. "They have the quaintest little grocery store." She frowned faintly. "I don't really know why, but the owner looked kinda relieved when Nate and I left."

Drake exchanged a glance with Callie and Haruki. The rest of them could hardly tell the two super soldiers that they came across as cold and extremely dangerous upon first impression.

"So, where is this gate of yours?" Artemus asked Sebastian testily.

"I cannot reveal that."

Artemus narrowed his eyes. "Why not?"

"Because it is safe where it is right now and the fewer people who know its location, the better," Sebastian said, a stubborn note creeping into his voice.

Artemus raked his hair irritably with his fingers. "Alright, if you won't tell us where it is, can you at least say what form it's in? Like we told you before, Callie's was an arch and Haruki's a mirror."

"I cannot divulge that either."

Artemus scowled.

"Uh-oh," Serena murmured to Nate. "Goldilocks looks like he's about to pop a fuse again."

Sebastian hesitated in the face of Artemus's hot glare. "All I can tell you is that I found it quite accidentally ten years ago. Just as my pocket watch drew me in and resonated with my beast, we experienced the diametrically opposite reaction in its presence. We could both tell it was evil."

"You said it was only part of your gate though." Drake frowned. "Do you know where the other half is?"

"I—" Sebastian faltered. "I am not sure."

Haruki stared. "Not being sure means you think you have an idea where it might be."

"Maybe," Sebastian murmured.

"You take cryptic to a whole other level, don't you?" Artemus said with a disgusted look.

Sebastian ignored him, seemingly lost in his own thoughts.

"We knew when we came across it that we needed to hide it somewhere secure," he said, staring at his hands. "Demons were bound to be attracted by its presence." He looked up. "My beast gave me instructions as to how to conceal it in such a way that demons could not see it."

A blast of intuition bolted through Drake. "Does it have anything to do with iron?"

The others shot him surprised looks.

"Remember what William Boone said about demons and iron?" Drake reminded them. "That it repulses them somehow?"

"Oh yeah," Callie murmured.

"Haruki's gate was in an iron strongbox too," Serena said.

Haruki frowned. "That's right."

Unease clouded Sebastian's eyes. "Is William Boone Otis's father?"

"Yes," Artemus said.

"He is correct," Sebastian said slowly. "About iron repelling demons. My beast recommended we shield the piece of my gate we discovered with it."

Serena raised an eyebrow. "You know, if the Vatican finds out you're holding onto part of a gate to Hell, they're gonna want to get their hands on it."

Sebastian's expression grew chilly. "And if I refuse?"

"If you refuse, we will stand by you and defend you," Callie stated resolutely.

Sebastian blinked, astonishment widening his eyes slightly.

"You are one of us," Callie said flatly. She looked around the room before focusing on Sebastian. "More importantly, you are my and Smokey's brother. The links between us and our beasts are unbreakable. None but God himself can undo our bonds."

Drake stared. It was unusual for Callie to be so serious.

He knew she meant every word she had just said, though. Because it felt true. To all of them.

Their bonds *were* unbreakable.

Color stained Sebastian's cheekbones as he gazed at his sister; he looked flustered for a moment.

He finally regained his composure, cleared his throat, and murmured a quiet, "Thank you."

Artemus sighed. "Well, now that we've decided we might declare war on Rome one day, what's our next move?"

Sebastian removed the faded tarot piece from his vest pocket, his expression growing determined. "We find the tavern referred to on this card."

ELTON FROWNED AT THE MAN ON THE SCREEN OF HIS smartband. "Are you certain?"

"Yes," Raoul Peirce replied with a decisive nod. "It's another area that has been of concern to our group for some time, but we never managed to pinpoint the exact location of interest. The incidents reported in the last few hours are a pretty strong indication that this is the place." The man hesitated. "Thank you again for the information concerning Oxford. I've heard of Artemus Steele and his unit of elite operatives on the Vatican grapevine. I believe their abilities are quite a sight to behold."

Elton masked a grimace. "They are formidable, but more like a group of excitable kids with superpowers on a sugar rush than the black-ops agents you're envisioning."

Peirce's face fell. "Oh."

The news the man had just imparted troubled Elton and for more than one reason. Elton had called the

London Vatican group leader to tell him what Artemus and the others had discovered in the tunnels under Oxford. Peirce, in turn, had apprised him of disturbing events currently unfolding in the territory under his jurisdiction. Elton could not help but feel that these new incidents were somehow linked to Cunningham's attack on Artemus's shop and Otis's disappearance.

"Can you send me the details of where your operation will take place tonight?"

Confusion washed across Peirce's face. "Sure. But it will be too late for you to get here to assist us, if that is your intention."

"It isn't. Artemus and the others are still in England. Trust me, they're gonna wanna know about this."

Elton ended the call, pulled up Artemus's number, and drummed his fingers on his desk as he listened to the dial tone. A click finally sounded at the other end of the line.

"Hello?"

"It's me again," Elton said curtly. "I have some news. Something is happening in London. I just spoke to their Vatican group leader. I think whatever is going on over there may be linked to Cunningham and Otis."

"Wait, I'll put you on speaker." A low drone of voices came through the smartband's speakers in the next instant. "You're talking to everyone."

"There have been several disturbances in an area of the city that the Vatican Group has been concerned about for a while. It's in the West End, close to—"

"Let me guess," Artemus interrupted. "Covent Garden?"

Elton stilled. "How did you know that?"

"We're looking at it on Serena's computer right now." There was a protracted pause. "She and Haruki, er, may or may not have hacked into the Vatican group's communications network."

Elton stopped drumming his fingers. "What?!"

"Like I said," Artemus continued breezily, "may or may not. By the way, have you seen this place on a map?"

Elton scowled. "Serena, Haruki, and I need to have a serious conversation about security when you guys get back. And no, I haven't."

"Serena's sending you a screenshot right now."

Elton's smartband pinged. An image appeared on his screen. "I see it."

"It was Haruki who suggested the next step," Artemus said. "Here's the most relevant screenshot. It took a moment to line it up, but it fits."

Elton's stomach dropped when he saw the second image. "Wait. Is that—?"

"It's the Tower, the tarot card Smokey discovered in Oxford, with 'The Drunken Minstrel' written on the back. Haruki suggested we superimpose it across the locations of all the pubs we found by that name in England. We just started looking at the London ones when the incident alerts came up."

Elton's heart thumped rapidly against his ribs. The other symbol on the screen was undeniable. And it was one he'd seen before.

It was the Sigil of Baphomet, perfectly silhouetted by the streets and intersections of that part of London. And the tavern—the origin of the suspected demonic events taking place right now—was dead in the center of it.

CHAPTER TWENTY-NINE

DUSK WAS FALLING WHEN THEY REACHED THE OUTSKIRTS of London. They headed toward Whitechapel, passed the Tower of London, and followed the Thames to the Victoria Embankment.

Traffic died down when they got within a mile of Covent Garden. Artemus and the others had seen the news on Serena's computer before they'd set off; a major incident had been declared in the West End and the area had been evacuated, with locals being advised to stay away by the city's mayor and emergency services.

The official story was that it was a gas leak. The authorities could hardly admit to the terrifying truth. Which was that a gang of monsters from man's worst nightmares had just killed a whole bunch of people in a frenzied attack, before apparently retreating inside a pub to hide.

They came to a police cordon. Sebastian slowed to a stop and rolled the window down. An officer approached their vehicle.

"We are expected," Sebastian told her.

The officer studied them warily. "Are you folks the environmental specialists we've been waiting for?"

"Yes," Sebastian replied blithely.

The woman looked over at the second SUV, noted their number plates, and nodded them onward. "Turn left at the next intersection. The rest of your team is waiting at the end of the road, in a car park."

They drove through the cordon and followed her directions.

Artemus leaned forward and stared through the SUV's windshield. "You seeing this?"

Sebastian studied the dark haze shrouding the air ahead of them with a frown.

"I hope these guys we're meeting have respirators," Serena said from the backseat.

"I do not think we will need them," Sebastian murmured.

He felt Artemus, Serena, and Drake's stares on his face.

"Why?" Drake asked.

"Because I am pretty sure I know what that is," Sebastian said, his voice hardening.

Though they were far away from the fog, he could detect a familiar smell of decay.

They found the leader of the London Vatican group and a team of some fifty agents waiting for them in an underground garage.

"Raoul Peirce?" Artemus said to the dark-haired man with the goatee who approached them when they got out of their vehicles.

"Indeed." Peirce shook Artemus's hand and greeted the others with nods. "It's a pleasure to finally meet your group. We've heard a lot about you in the last few months."

He indicated the Vatican agents behind him. The men and women were watching Artemus and the others with a mixture of awe and mild suspicion. Their eyes widened slightly when they registered Smokey's presence by Artemus's feet. The rabbit's chocolate fur blended in with the gloom shrouding the parking lot.

Peirce paled slightly as he gazed at the bunny. "Is that the, er, hellhound?"

"His name is Smokey," Callie said.

"You can pet him if you like," Haruki added.

Smokey's eyes flashed red. He huffed a warning at the Yakuza heir.

"What?" Haruki shrugged at Artemus's frown. "I'm trying to break the awkward social tension of our meet-and-greet."

Artemus sighed and turned to Peirce. "Have there been any further demon sightings since the last reported one?"

"No. We haven't been able to approach the main incident area since that awful smog came down over the place. I've never seen anything like it before. A number of the public have been admitted to hospital with breathing difficulties and loss of consciousness." Peirce turned to one of the agents. "We have some protective masks for you to wear."

Artemus cocked a thumb at Sebastian. "He says we won't need it."

Low murmurs rose from the Vatican agents.

Peirce frowned at Artemus and Sebastian. "What do you mean?"

"Oh." Callie brightened up. "Is it that toxic vapor Cunningham released back in Chicago, when you and

Artemus fought him? The one you cleared with a sphere of divine energy?"

Sebastian dipped his chin. "Yes, it is."

Peirce's face became blank. "Divine energy?"

"How about we get going and you can see it all in action?" Artemus told the Vatican branch leader.

They gathered their weapons and headed out of the parking lot.

"Why does she have a walking stick?" one the agents whispered behind them. "And have you seen that guy's gun?"

Callie looked over her shoulder. "Oh, this?" She raised her cane. "It's the Scepter of Gabriel." Light flashed along the staff as it transformed. "His weapon has a prayer on it written by Zaqiel, the fifteenth leader of the Grigori." She indicated the firearm in Artemus's hand. "It can send demons back to Hell."

The agents gaped, their eyes locked on the scepter.

"Show off," Serena muttered.

Callie smiled impishly.

Shadows engulfed them as they started up the main road, the glare of the streetlights dulled by the miasma clouding the air. The sound of traffic was a distant, muffled drone. Their footsteps echoed eerily on the blacktop.

The stench of decomposition grew steadily stronger.

Artemus stopped a moment later and glanced at Sebastian. "About here?"

Sebastian nodded. "Yes."

They had reached a thick fringe of fog. From the way his throat was feeling, he knew it would soon start to physically affect them. He removed his gloves and brought forth a glowing sphere of energy in his right hand.

Gasps rose from the Vatican agents.

Sebastian ignored them, took out his pocket watch, and released the golden whip, the weapon's form manifesting with greater ease than it had the first time he had used it.

Artemus and Drake unleashed their holy swords.

Haruki and Callie morphed into their divine beast forms, Haruki's bracelet flashing red and gold before transforming into the Flaming Sword of Camael.

Smokey shook himself and grew rapidly in size, his fur shrinking to a glossy, black hide as he adopted his first hellhound shape, a low growl rumbling from his powerful chest.

Serena and Nate activated their liquid-armor suits and took out their blades.

Peirce swallowed audibly.

Static filled the atmosphere. The sphere in Sebastian's hand grew in size and brilliance as he poured more power into it, to the point it almost dazzled the Vatican agents. Strands of light forked out from the pulsing globe when he started walking ahead of their group, the radiant beams sucking in the currents of poison wreathing the air until they vanished into nothingness.

The shadows lightened ahead.

They had just passed the Royal Opera House when the first demons appeared in their path.

CHAPTER THIRTY

"HERE THEY COME," ARTEMUS WARNED, HIS GRIP tightening on his gun and sword.

The demons charged toward them, their talons raising sparks as they bounded and leaped across the asphalt, their obsidian eyes filled with hate.

Artemus and the Vatican agents fired into the horde.

Some of the demons slowed, their momentum broken by the silver-leaded bullets that slammed into them. Two of them let out unholy screeches before bursting into flames, bodies disintegrating into ashes when Artemus's shots found their mark.

Then, the creatures were upon them.

Artemus stabbed a demon in the gut, shot another one in the face, and kicked a third one in the groin. Sebastian's whip cracked next to him, the lissome lash glimmering sinuously through the air before slicing a demon's head clean off. His eyes glowed white as he cast lighting balls at another two, the spheres blasting giant, gaping holes into the creatures' chests.

Fire roared to Artemus's left in a blinding jet that

engulfed three demons, the flames so close they almost singed the hairs on his arm. He looked over his shoulder and narrowed his eyes at Callie and Haruki.

The Chimera pointed at the Colchian Dragon. "That was him."

Haruki grimaced guiltily, steam curling from his jaws. "Sorry. I got a bit excited."

"He can breathe fire?!" Peirce shouted in a shocked voice from where he and a group of agents were fighting four demons.

"Yeah," Artemus said, disgruntled. "So can Callie."

Callie grinned. The golden snake sprouting from the base of her spine batted away a demon creeping up behind her.

They fought their way steadily through the horde and were soon rid of the creatures. Eerie silence fell around them as they pressed on toward their target. Unease coiled through Artemus a short while later.

That was too easy.

Something made him glance over his shoulder. The hairs rose on his arms. He stopped and turned. The others paused and looked around.

"What the hell is that?" Haruki muttered.

Several Vatican agents stumbled back in alarm.

An inky darkness was closing in slowly in their wake, deadening their footfall and obscuring the path they had just travelled.

It wasn't the toxic fog that was sucking out the light behind them.

"Sebastian?" Artemus said quietly.

"I know," Sebastian murmured grimly.

The sphere of light in his hand intensified, its radiance keeping the shadows encircling them at bay. They were past the point where they could retreat. Their only option was to keep going.

They forged ahead and reached a junction some two hundred feet from the tavern.

Sebastian froze.

Artemus halted and followed his gaze to the murky rooftop of the building to their left. His pulse jumped.

The color drained from Peirce's face. "Shit."

Serena frowned. "It's a trap."

Artemus clenched his jaw. A sea of yellow eyes glowed atop the edifices flanking them on four sides.

There were at least a hundred demons surrounding them.

His knuckles whitened on the hilt of his sword. None of them had sensed the creatures' foul energy growing around them. Which meant that the darkness had been meant to mask the demons' approach in more ways than one.

"We have to split up." Lines marred Sebastian's brow as he gazed at the road north of the intersection. "It is the only way we can reach the tavern and Cunningham."

Artemus scowled. "Is that where he is?"

A muscle twitched in Sebastian's jawline. "Yes. His stench is strongest from that direction."

Drake frowned. "They're probably banking on us doing exactly that."

"I agree," Serena said. "Whatever their motive is for setting this ambush, they mean to divide us."

"I think our time for thinking this through just ran out!" Haruki warned.

Artemus cursed. The demons were coming down from the rooftops, their monstrous forms moving lithely along the vertical facades of the buildings.

"I'll stay here with Haruki and Nate!" Callie said, her eyes flashing jade green with power. "You five take the tavern!"

Artemus hesitated.

"We need to go, now!" Sebastian snarled.

"Damn it!" Artemus snapped.

He glared at the approaching demons before bolting toward the tavern, Sebastian, Drake, Serena, and Smokey at his side.

"I feel bad leaving them," Serena said grimly.

Artemus cast a final look at the intersection behind them as they neared a turn in the road. A mass of demons filled the space, their bodies a writhing cloud of impenetrable darkness. He could see no sign of Nate, the divine beasts, or the Vatican agents.

"They're strong." Drake exchanged a tense glance with him. "They can defeat those demons."

The Drunken Minstrel finally came into view. They staggered to a stop in front of the building. Marble pillars with gilded heads spanned the width of the tavern's facade, the columns supporting elaborate architraves decorated with Victorian ornaments. They could see no light through the thick, mullioned windows framing the entrance.

Artemus reached for the door handle.

"Wait," Drake said. "Let me go first."

"Why?"

"Listen to me, for once!" Drake snapped. "They won't hurt me. I'm too important to Ba'al."

Smokey looked anxiously between them, a low whine escaping his jowls.

Artemus clenched his teeth and gazed into Drake's eyes. However much he wanted to deny it, his twin was right. He finally conceded defeat with a sigh.

"Go ahead."

Drake took the lead as they walked inside the tavern. They paused on the threshold, senses on high alert.

A long, polished, oak counter ran down the bar on their right. The dull gleam of glass came from the bottles lining the shelves behind it and the glassware suspended from hanging racks. Leather-padded booths and stools framed the tables crowding the floor to their left, leaving a narrow passageway that led toward an opening at the back.

The place was dead. There was no one around.

Light flared in Sebastian's right hand. He released the glowing sphere floating above his palm. It levitated toward the ceiling, dispelling some of the gloom.

Floorboards creaked somewhere above them. Artemus stiffened.

"They're on the second floor," Serena murmured.

"The stairs are at the back," Drake said, heading in that direction.

They found the staircase at the end of a dark passage. A frayed runner muted their approach as they took the steps to the second floor.

A corridor appeared at the top. There were five doors opening off it.

They cleared the washrooms on the left, and the office and staff lounge on the right. The last door was the function room at the very end of the passage.

"He is in there," Sebastian said darkly.

Even Artemus could not miss the repulsive odor creeping from under the doorway in front of them. It was the same rank scent that had permeated the air around Cunningham back at the antique shop in Chicago.

Drake closed his hand on the doorknob and glanced at them.

Serena's knuckles whitened on her blades. The glowing sphere of divine light in Sebastian's right hand grew brighter and the golden whip in his left hand rose slightly, as if to sniff the air for the demons it wished to destroy. Smokey grew by another couple of feet, his eyes shifting from red to yellow as his power surged.

Artemus put his gun away and grasped his sword in a double-handed grip. They would be fighting in close confines and he didn't want to risk accidentally hitting the others with a bullet. He dipped his chin at his brother.

Drake opened the door.

CHAPTER THIRTY-ONE

THE ATTACK WAS IMMEDIATE AND SAVAGE.

Serena glimpsed motion on her left and leaned sharply out of the way of the enormous fist coming at her face. The blow glanced off her skull, making her ears ring. She twisted on her heels and drove her dagger into her attacker's flank.

Her blade bounced off rock-hard skin.

Serena looked up into her assailant's liquid-silver eyes. It was a first-generation super soldier.

Shit! He's in demon form!

Artemus swore as he narrowly escaped disembowelment by two sets of wicked, metal talons. "You don't happen to have one of those EMP devices on you by any chance, do you?!"

"No! Nate's got them!"

Serena cursed herself for her lack of insight. She should have grabbed one of the devices Gideon had given her from Nate. She blocked a kick inches from her left thigh and clenched her jaw when the impact jarred her bones.

These assholes are strong.

Serena sprung back out of her attacker's reach and glanced around. They were surrounded by ten super soldier demons. Drake's blade and Sebastian's whip were proving as useless against the creatures as Artemus's sword and Smokey's fangs and claws. Though they were managing to keep their adversaries at bay, they could not eliminate them. She frowned.

Of Cunningham there was no sign.

"Where is he?" Sebastian growled, his gaze searching the shadowy corners of the function room frantically while he pushed back at a super soldier demon with a sphere of energy. "I can smell him!"

"I don't know!" Artemus said with a scowl, blocking a punch to his head with his sword.

Serena bobbed beneath the fist of the super soldier demon coming at her, grabbed hold of his wrist, and scaled the wall behind her backward with her feet. The creature followed her with his gaze, his blank stare analyzing her movements.

She grinned fiercely, sprung off the wall, and vaulted over his head. She landed behind him with a thud, yanked on his arm, and flipped him up and over with a grunt. His eyes widened a moment before he crashed onto his front before her, the floorboards caving and splintering beneath him.

Metal gleamed on her left. Serena grabbed the wrist of the super soldier demon aiming his claws at her eye and wrenched it backward savagely. A loud crack sounded as she broke the bones in his forearm.

Serena blinked, shocked. *Is this what Sebastian meant?*

She could feel it now. A warm energy spreading through her flesh and blood. Power buzzed in her veins as the heat intensified, the nanorobots in her body responding to the sudden surge in her physical abilities.

Damn. This is—

"Interesting," someone murmured behind her.

Serena whirled around. A gasp left her lips. She froze.

Her gaze dropped slowly from the man who stood scrutinizing her as if she were a lab rat to the round, pointed blade that had just impaled her right flank. The weapon protruded from her attacker's very hand and gleamed as if it were alive.

Nanorobots!

"You'll do," Cunningham said with a smile.

Serena heard Drake shout out her name. She felt a tug.

Cunningham was stepping back into the narrow rift he had appeared from. The blade embedded in her flesh dragged her forward.

Serena grabbed the weapon desperately with her hands and started pulling it out of her body, blood gushing thickly from her wound and splattering onto the floor. She inhaled sharply as the end of the blade sprouted vicious hooks that stabbed into her back, anchoring it in place.

Crimson darkness swallowed her as she fell inside the rift after Cunningham.

DRAKE BOLTED TOWARD THE FISSURE AS IT STARTED TO close.

"*No!*" Artemus yelled behind him.

Drake ignored his twin, gritted his teeth, and leapt through the shrinking portal. It closed behind him with a clap of thunder.

There was a sensation of speed and a stomach-churning feeling of weightlessness.

A thousand screaming voices tore through Drake's ears as he drifted swiftly through a pitch-black space throbbing with a bright, scarlet light. Vague shapes appeared in the distance around him, their gruesome forms highlighted sporadically by crimson pulses of illumination. Drake shuddered as he glimpsed mouths open on agonizing shrieks and hands gouging out eyes and tearing at flesh. He could not tell if the figures were humans or demons.

Is this Hell?!

A point of light appeared up ahead and grew rapidly.

Air whooshed out of Drake's lips as he tumbled out of the other side of the rift. He landed on his side on a cold, stone floor, rolled, and sprung into a low crouch, his shield and blade ready. His breath froze in his lungs the next instant.

He was atop some kind of turret. Narrow steps spiraled down ahead of him to a large, round tower teeming with demons some twenty feet below. An icy wind blew over the ramparts on his left and brought with it the smell of the sea. A million stars dotted the cloudless night sky above him as far as the horizon.

But it wasn't his location or the presence of the horde of fiends that captured Drake's undivided attention. It was the figures at the far end of the tower who held his unblinking gaze.

Otis stood with his hands fisted and his back against a stone wall. Though his face was ashen, his eyes blazed more with anger than fear.

Serena was on her knees in front of him, her hands locked around the wrist of the man who clutched her throat in an iron grip, a fearsome scowl darkening her features despite the blood pooling beneath her and the talons scraping red lines into her skin.

Cunningham stood above the super soldier in his human form, the wicked blade in his right hand poised an inch from her left eye.

"If you do not agree to translate those journals, I will tear her eyes out," the demon told Otis in a calm voice, as if he were discussing the weather. "Then, I will slice her ears and tongue while you watch. After that, I will rip her limbs clean off her body one by one before carving out her internal organs." He smiled at Otis. "If that still does not convince you to acquiesce to our demands, I will kidnap one of your other friends and do the same to them."

Serena turned her head with some difficulty and looked Otis in the eye. "Whatever this bastard wants you to do, don't do it! Artemus and the others are on their way! They'll—"

A harsh sound left Serena. She bit her lower lip until it bled and glared at the man who had just stabbed her in her left shoulder.

Cunningham bared his teeth and tightened his hold on her neck. He twisted the blade in her new wound. Serena hissed in pain, the sound leaving her with a choked noise.

Drake heard metal grind against bone even from where he crouched.

A red mist filled his vision.

He didn't know if his presence had gone undetected thus far because the energy inside him resembled that of the demons. Even if that was the case, he didn't care.

The rage that had been building inside him in the last few seconds exploded into full-blown bloodlust. His wings

trembled and unfurled. Black armor sprouted across his
skin and clothes, encasing his frame. His blade thickened
and lengthened into a broadsword, edges morphing into
jagged teeth that smoldered with fire. Red runes sprung to
life on his darkening shield.

Power flooded Drake as he released his inner demon.

CHAPTER THIRTY-TWO

A POWERFUL DETONATION BOOMED ACROSS THE TOWER, sending the demonic crowd filling the stone floor scattering. Surprise dawned on Cunningham's face. He started to turn. Then, he was gone, his body sailing through the air before crashing into the creatures behind him, his blade ripped straight out of her flesh.

Serena grunted and clamped a hand to the wound in her left shoulder.

"Oh God," Otis mumbled.

Serena followed his gaze. Her breath caught.

Drake stood before them in his dark angel form. His pupils glowed with the light of Hell as he frowned down at her and Otis. Flames danced on his right hand, where he curled his fingers into a fist around the hilt of his serrated broadsword.

Serena's hands dropped instinctively to the sheaths on her thighs. They were empty, her blades long lost during her passage through the rift.

Drake followed her movement with his gaze, his scowl deepening.

Pain twisted Serena's heart. She could see a battle raging inside his eyes and knew he was fighting to control his inner demon. She climbed unsteadily to her feet, conscious of the blood still coursing freely from her injuries; her body wasn't healing as it should and she was hemorrhaging internally.

"Dra—"

"Son of Samyaza." Cunningham had risen from where he lay and stood studying Drake with a guarded expression. A shudder ran through him. His body shifted and swelled, adopting his monstrous demon form. He took a step toward them, pupils flaring with ochre brightness. "We were not expecting you."

Drake turned to look at him.

Cunningham stiffened and stilled at whatever he saw on the dark angel's face. "Can we not convince you to join our side? After all, *this* is where you belong." The demon indicated the fiends behind him before extending a hand to Drake. "This is where you have always belonged, Son of Samyaza. You are the bearer of your father's soul. It is your birthright and your Fate to join our circle."

Drake froze. Otis drew a sharp breath.

Surprise jolted Serena. *Samyaza is the demon inside Drake?!*

Drake was still for a timeless moment. Flames flared on his broadsword. Serena's eyes widened when he lifted the weapon and spread his wings protectively in front of her and Otis.

"I will decide my own Fate, demon."

Serena blinked as Drake's voice reverberated menacingly around the tower, making the very air tremble. She could feel his power surging even more.

Someone clamped a hand on her right flank. She looked down.

Otis had torn the sleeve off his shirt and was pressing the wad of cloth to her wound. "Lean on me. You look like you're about to fall."

Serena hesitated before looping an arm around his shoulders. A wave of dizziness washed over her.

She had never felt so weak in her life.

Cunningham frowned at Drake. "Then, so be it. We will bring you down and drag you to Hell ourselves, so you may face your father and the Council."

His words were a signal to the demons on the tower.

Amber eyes flared in the gloom. The creatures charged toward them as one, their voices rising to deafening shrieks.

ARTEMUS GASPED AND BENT OVER. HE DROPPED TO THE floor on one knee, his wings wrapping around his body like a shield while he clutched his chest.

"What is the matter?" Sebastian asked, alarmed.

He rushed over to Artemus, the last super soldier demon falling behind him, the creature's legs crumbling under the massive lightning-ball assault he had just unleashed.

Smokey trembled where he stood in his Cerberus form to Artemus's right. He let go of the body of the dead super soldier demon in his jaws, lifted his heads, and released an unholy howl that rattled the windows.

Artemus's heart throbbed as the agonizing sound echoed through him. He knew the hellhound was experiencing the same torment tearing through his very bones.

"It's Drake!" He lifted his head and gazed beseechingly at Sebastian. "I—he's in his dark angel form! And the demon inside him is growing stronger!"

Mere minutes had passed since his twin had vanished into the rift with Serena and Cunningham. It was only after Artemus and Smokey had adopted their final forms and Sebastian's attacks had grown more tenacious that they had finally managed to overcome the super soldier demons.

Blood pounded dully in Artemus's skull. He could feel the emotions swirling through his brother, wherever he was. Drake was fighting demons and he had unleashed his own devil in order to do so. Beneath the rage and blood-lust swamping his twin, Artemus could feel the monster pushing inch by inch against the barriers of his eternal prison.

"We have to find him." He rose to his feet and gripped his broadsword, desperation surging through him. "Smokey and I *need* to be with Drake! We are the only ones who can stop him from fully succumbing to his demon!"

The door of the function room flew open. Callie, Haruki, Nate, Peirce, and the Vatican agents rushed in, weapons at the ready despite their various wounds, their breaths coming in short, sharp pants. They stumbled to a stop in the middle of the floor.

"What happened?" Callie asked, staring at the dead super soldier demons.

Nate's expression grew agitated as he searched the room with his gaze. "Where's Serena?"

Haruki looked around with a frown. "Drake's not here either."

Artemus swallowed. "Cunningham took Serena into a rift. Drake followed them."

"What?!" Callie gasped.

Shocked murmurs rose from the Vatican agents.

"I have to inform my superiors about this," Peirce mumbled. "We—"

"We do not have the leisure of time," Sebastian interrupted coolly. "We have to go. Now."

Artemus turned to Sebastian, wild hope bursting to life in his heart.

"Go where?" Haruki said.

"To where they are." Sebastian met Artemus's eyes. "I think I can open a rift to their location."

Callie's mouth opened and closed for a soundless moment. "How?! I thought only demons could create those!"

"I was close enough to Cunningham this time to get a sense of how he did it. I should be able to copy his technique with divine energy." Sebastian glanced from Artemus to Smokey and back. "More to the point, I have you two at hand."

"What do you mean?" Haruki said.

A bolt of intuition danced through Artemus. "It's because of our connection." He looked at the others, fingers clenching on his sword. "The bond that links Smokey and me to Drake!"

Sebastian nodded. "Yes. Now, if you will excuse me."

He closed the distance to Artemus and laid a hand on his chest.

Artemus startled.

Sebastian's eyes blazed with power. A sphere of pure, white light exploded into existence in his right hand.

This close, Artemus could feel the heat pulsing off the lightning ball.

Smokey padded over and nudged Artemus's fingers with his snouts. Artemus touched his middle head and closed his eyes. Heat poured through him across their bond, a wave of energy that resonated with his soul.

A pair of hands landed softly on Artemus's back.

"We are all connected," Callie murmured.

"Indeed we are," Haruki said.

The light in Sebastian's hand and eyes brightened further as the Chimera and the Colchian Dragon's life forces merged with theirs. He released the sphere. It rose in the air, a throbbing star of power.

"*Reveal.*"

CHAPTER THIRTY-THREE

DRAKE SWUNG HIS BLADE. THE SWORD SANG THROUGH the air and decapitated five demons, flames flickering wildly on its jagged edges. The creatures' bodies exploded into ash. More demons appeared through the falling cinders. Drake bared his teeth and snarled, the stone floor cracking beneath his feet as his power swelled.

He could feel the devil rising inside him. The one he now knew was his own father. The demon who had sired him and who wished one day to take over his human body. The fiend responsible for his wretched Fate.

Drake gritted his teeth. *I will not let you win!*

The demon raged as the cage keeping him captive stayed put, the walls holding fast under Drake's sheer will.

Sweat beaded Drake's forehead. Though he was managing to hold the demon horde at bay, he did not know how much longer he would be able to do so, nor how much time he had left before his own devil's prison crumbled.

A disgusted sound left Cunningham. The demon commander had so far not participated in the battle and stood at the back of the crowd of creatures amassed before Drake, his cold eyes analyzing the fight critically.

"I see I shall have to step in and sully my hands," the demon growled, glancing at his army with an expression of loathing.

Black wings unfurled from Cunningham's back with a loud thump. He flexed his talons.

Drake's pulse stuttered.

A thick whip made of glittering metal had just sprouted from the demon's right hand.

A rift tore open next to Cunningham. He reached inside it and removed a dark broadsword that glowed red at the edges.

Drake stared. The blade was similar to his own weapon.

Shit.

∿

"Damn!" Serena muttered.

"That's not good, is it?" Otis said hoarsely.

Serena clenched her jaw. She was surprised that Drake had managed to maintain control over his inner devil for so long. The last time he'd fought like this, against a powerful demon commander, he had fallen prey to the bloodlust in his veins and surrendered to his dark side within minutes.

"We have to help him," Otis mumbled.

Serena looked at Otis where he propped her up. Something was different about Artemus's assistant. For one thing, she'd realized that it wasn't just Drake who was protecting them from the demons. A few of the creatures had climbed over the battlements and outer wall of the tower to try and creep up behind them, but to no avail.

There was some kind of force keeping them at bay. A force that was only evident when they came within arm's reach of where Otis and Serena stood.

It was as if an invisible barrier was holding the demons back.

Serena stiffened. *What the—?*

Warmth was slowly spreading through her body from where Otis was touching her.

"Is that you?"

Otis dragged his gaze from where Drake fought Cunningham and blinked at Serena. "Is that me what?"

Serena swallowed as the heat intensified. Something was healing her. Her nanorobots, disabled by whatever it was Cunningham had done to her when he stabbed her with his weapon, were coming back to life. A shiver raced down her spine as power flooded her.

This is more than healing!

Serena removed the bloodied bandage from the wound on her flank. The gaping hole was closing at an accelerated rate, faster than she'd ever been able to achieve before. Golden sparks danced through her healing flesh before the skin and armor closed over. She looked at her hands and saw a faint shimmer of the same energy spark across her fingertips.

Serena stared at Otis. "It *is* you."

Whatever Otis was, he was brimming with divine energy. And it was resonating with the threads of holy power that had seeped inside her body and her blood in the last few months of co-existing with Artemus and the others.

A savage sound ripped the air ahead of them,

distracting her. A cloud of darkness had erupted around Drake.

Cunningham smiled fiercely. "Yield to Samyaza, dark angel. It is your Fate!"

"*It is NOT my Fate!*" Drake roared.

Fear wrapped icy fingers around Serena's soul. Drake's demon was winning.

"We have to help him," Otis repeated, his face pale.

Serena gritted her teeth. "How? If we go anywhere near them right now, we'll be ripped to shreds!"

Touch him.

Serena froze. She looked around wildly. "Did you hear that?"

"Did I hear what?" Otis said.

Touch him, both of you. And bind the demon.

Otis startled and glanced behind them. "Who said that?"

Serena shivered as the woman's voice echoed inside her skull. The words were more than just a suggestion. They were a command. She took a shaky breath.

"Stay with me," she told Otis.

"Why? What are you—?"

She grabbed his left hand, closed the distance to Drake, and placed their fingers on the dark angel's back.

OTIS GASPED.

The tower had vanished the moment he and Serena made physical contact with Drake. In its stead was darkness. A darkness so complete he wondered fleetingly if he'd taken a blow to the head and lost consciousness.

Footsteps sounded in the shadows to his right. He turned and saw Serena.

"This way."

She took the lead and headed into the gloom.

Otis stared as he fell into step behind her. A glow surrounded Serena. Her skin and hair were alight with a faint, golden haze. He looked down at his hands and blinked in surprise. The same radiance was brightening his flesh.

Something flickered in the darkness up ahead. A distorted, writhing shape that appeared and disappeared from view. Otis's eyes rounded as they drew closer to the strange phenomenon.

It was Drake. But also, not Drake. He stood frozen to the ground, his figure blurring as his body alternated rapidly between his dark angel form and a huge, fearsome demon with hateful red eyes.

At their feet, shining like a beacon in the darkness, was a golden rope.

Take it.

Otis jumped and whirled around. A figure stood in twilight some dozen feet from them. It was a woman wearing a white dress, with long hair so pale it glowed in the darkness. He could not make out her features but for her eyes.

They sparkled like the very Heavens.

"Who are you?" Serena said softly.

The super soldier had turned to face the stranger.

Take the rope and bind him.

Otis stared. He was certain the woman's lips had not moved.

Serena frowned. "Not until you tell us—"

I am Drake and Artemus's mother. And right now, he needs you more than he needs me. Both of you.

Otis drew a sharp breath.

A wave of sadness washed over him, so intense and heavy he almost crumpled to his knees. He blinked sudden tears from his eyes and knew instinctively that he was feeling the sorrow of the woman who stood watching them. Serena's hands fisted by her sides, her expression telling Otis she had just experienced the same flood of emotion.

The stranger looked past them to Drake.

That child is brave, but he is losing this battle.

Her unearthly gaze moved to them once more.

You must help him before all is lost.

Her eyes lingered on Serena.

The super soldier held the woman's stare for a timeless moment before turning to scrutinize the shape that was Drake and Samyaza locked in a battle of wills.

"Together," Serena said quietly.

Otis nodded.

They walked over to the golden rope and took one end each. Then they circled the dark angel and his fiend, looping the divine lasso around their melded bodies twice, their own fingers aglow with the holy light that shimmered on the restraint.

The demon let out a hiss of rage.

Drake threw his head back and screamed, his eyes flaring gold and red.

CHAPTER THIRTY-FOUR

THEY EMERGED ATOP A TURRET FLANKING ONE END OF A round tower.

"I think I'm going to be sick," Peirce mumbled, a hand over his mouth.

Several Vatican agents staggered to a nearby wall and threw up violently.

"That was pretty interesting," Haruki muttered, pale-faced.

Artemus's stomach still roiled from their passage through the rift.

It had taken Sebastian several minutes to open a breach in the same spot where Cunningham's portal had vanished. He'd led the way into the dark, hellish space beyond the crimson fissure and followed the thread of energy that connected Artemus and Smokey to Drake all the way to the other side.

There was no time to ponder the ghastly things they had just witnessed.

Because standing at the far end of the tower below

them, surrounded by an army of demons and the remains
of dozens of others, were Drake, Serena, and Otis.

Artemus's breath caught.

Just as he'd suspected, Drake was in his dark angel
mode, his eyes aglow with a violent red light, his body
shrouded in a mantle of darkness. Serena and Otis stood
behind him, their hands on his back while he fought
Cunningham. Artemus stared.

A strange radiance emanated from their fingers where
they made contact with Drake.

Even from the distance, he could tell it was divine
energy that they were wielding. The same divine energy
Sebastian manipulated to create his lightning balls and the
force that gave all of them their powers.

A wave of bloodlust echoed across Artemus's bond
with Drake. Trepidation filled him. He could feel his twin
losing control as he battled the demon commander.

No! He's going to—

Drake stiffened. Gold flashed in his eyes, dampening
the crimson haze filling his gaze. He threw his head back
and screamed. The cloud of shadows around him swelled
before exploding into nothingness.

Cunningham saw his opening and moved in to attack.

"Oh no you don't!" Artemus snarled.

He and Smokey leapt just as the demon's broadsword
arced toward Drake's chest, its edges gleaming with an evil
red light. The hellhound landed heavily amidst the demon
horde below, crushing several under his powerful paws. He
sprung into the air once more, Artemus swooping
above him.

Metal clashed violently. Sparks erupted in the night.

Cunningham froze. The demon looked slowly from
where Artemus had blocked his blade with his own pale

broadsword, to Smokey where the latter had closed his jaws on the arm from which the nanorobot whip sprouted.

The demon scowled. "Well, this is inconvenient."

The hellhound growled, fangs dripping acid onto Cunningham's arm. The liquid sizzled and burned holes in the fiend's flesh. The wounds healed instantly, his skin glinting with a hint of the nanorobots within him.

An untamed smile twisted Cunningham's lips.

Artemus swore as the demon took a gargantuan breath and exhaled an evil black cloud, the fumes pooling out rapidly from his nostrils and mouth.

SEBASTIAN CLENCHED HIS JAW WHERE HE STOOD ON TOP of the turret. He unleashed his golden whip, drew a sphere of divine energy, and cast it at the dark miasma flooding the tower.

The lightning ball twisted and turned rapidly through the air, clearing the toxic vapor.

Jets of fire bloomed on either side of him and struck the poisonous mist with a roar. The smoke cleared.

The noxious fumes remained untouched.

He looked pointedly at the Colchian Dragon and the Chimera.

"It was worth a try," Haruki said.

Callie grimaced and shrugged.

"Here they come," Nate said in a hard voice.

Sebastian observed the demon swarm heading up the stone staircase and the walls of the turret toward them.

He clutched his whip and brought forth another divine sphere. "I believe it is time to kick some buttocks."

"Butt," Haruki said. "It's kick butt."

≈

CUNNINGHAM SCOWLED AT THE GROUP CROWDING THE upper tower. His gaze landed on the figure with the golden whip and the ball of light in his hand.

It is the fault of that blasted man! I should have killed him when I had the chance!

"Hey, asshole," someone said coldly. "Your fight's with us."

Cunningham turned. The white angel glared at him where he stood beside Cerberus, his wings spread open to anchor his stance, his broadsword shimmering with Heaven's holy flames as he raised it defensively.

Behind them, the battle that had been taking place inside the dark angel had ended. Samyaza's heir had resumed his human appearance and was being propped up by the super soldier woman and Otis Boone, his body trembling with exhaustion and his shield and blade hanging limply in his grasp.

Cunningham let out a sound of contempt. There was no point fighting this battle. His plan had failed, for now.

"Retreat!" he growled to his demons.

Rifts appeared around the tower. The fiendish mob slunk inside the portals and vanished.

≈

DRAKE LOWERED HIMSELF HEAVILY TO THE STONE FLOOR just as the last breach closed, his heart throbbing erratically.

"Are you alright?" Otis said anxiously.

Drake nodded shakily before looking up at him and Serena. He couldn't help but feel that something momentous had just happened. And that it had involved all three of them.

"What...was that?"

Otis blinked, uncertain. "Hmm. I'm not sure."

Serena hesitated. "It was your mother." She glanced at Otis before meeting Drake's shocked gaze. "She told us what to do to stop the devil from taking you over."

"What?" Artemus mumbled.

Drake's brother had changed back into his human form and stood gaping at them. The others arrived hastily behind him, the Vatican agents scanning the dark keep with anxious expressions.

"You met our mother?" Drake climbed unsteadily to his feet and glanced around the tower. "Is she here?!"

"No." Serena's face grew shuttered. "She was inside your soul."

Drake startled. A stark memory flashed before him. He raised a hand to his belly.

"Who was inside whose soul now?" Callie said, wide-eyed.

Drake could still feel the heat of the golden lasso Serena and Otis had used to bind his demon. "Wait. That was real?! And it was *inside* me?!"

"She can enter people's souls?" Haruki hissed to Nate out the corner of his mouth.

"I—" The super soldier faltered, his expression troubled. "I don't know."

"What did she look like?" Artemus strode up to Serena and Otis, his tone urgent with desperation. "Our mother. What did she look like?!"

"She was tall and—and slender," Otis stammered.

"She wore a white dress and had long, fair hair that

wrapped around her body like a cloak," Serena said. "We couldn't really see her face, but her eyes were like—"

"The light of the stars," Artemus and Drake breathed simultaneously, their faces shining with wonderment.

They froze before turning and staring at each other.

"Wait! You've met mom?!" Artemus barked.

"I didn't know she was our mom!" Drake retorted. "I thought she was, I don't know," he waved a hand, "—a figment of my imagination or something! When did you see her?"

"In New York, when I first transformed into my angel form," Artemus said promptly.

Drake swallowed. "That's where I met her too."

Artemus narrowed his eyes. "And you never mentioned it?"

Drake frowned. "Neither did you, asshole."

"I see the intimate moment of brotherly love has passed," Sebastian muttered.

Smokey huffed out a sigh beside him.

"We should leave this place." Peirce studied the empty tower warily. "We don't know when those demons will be back."

Artemus turned to Sebastian. "Do you think you can create a rift back to London?"

Surprise jolted Drake. "Is that how you got here? Wherever the hell here is."

"We're on an island in the Outer Hebrides, off the northeast coast of Scotland," Nate said.

The rest of them stared.

The super soldier pointed to his smart band. "This thing has very good GPS."

Peirce looked at his own device with a frown. "What satellite network are you using? Ours has no signal."

"It's—" Nate started.

"—a secret," Serena concluded. She assessed Sebastian with a thoughtful stare. "So, you can open rifts now?"

"It is a long story."

"It was cool," one of the Vatican agents mumbled. "All ethereal like."

"We can't leave," Otis said in a determined voice. "Not without my mother's journals. If they remain in Ba'al and Amaymon's possession, they may decipher the location of the other gates and keys before we do."

Artemus stared. "Who's Amaymon?"

"He's one of the eight sub-princes of Hell," Otis said. "Or, as I'm coming to understand, just Princes of Hell."

A muscle twitched in Sebastian's jawline. "He is the demon who possesses Cunningham?"

"Yes."

CHAPTER THIRTY-FIVE

THEY MOVED SWIFTLY THROUGH THE CASTLE, THEIR footsteps echoing eerily on the flagstone floors. Sebastian glanced uneasily at the abandoned chambers they passed. He could detect no trace of demonic energy in the building. This should have reassured him.

Except it didn't.

Cunningham was a devious man. Sebastian wouldn't put it past him to still be lurking in the shadows, ready to attack them through a rift at a moment's notice. He could tell from Artemus and the others' vigilant demeanor that they were of the same mind.

Otis led them across a courtyard and into the main castle keep.

The smell of decomposing flesh washed over them when they were ten feet in. Sebastian frowned. This wing was sumptuously furnished and looked to be Cunningham's primary base of operations. Clouds of flies swarmed the rafters and rooms they crossed. The stench of decay grew stronger. Several Vatican agents retched and gagged.

"Is that Cunningham's scent?" Artemus said stiffly.

Sebastian shook his head. "No. That is just rotting flesh."

"He told me the carcasses weren't human," Otis mumbled.

"I think he lied," Serena said in a hard voice.

Otis paled and swallowed. "We're almost there."

They turned a corner and came to a thickset door. Otis stopped in front of it and turned the handle. Sebastian faltered in his steps beside Artemus and Callie.

Otis pushed the door open and entered Cunningham's study.

Thump.

A strange feeling of dread churned Sebastian's stomach as he slowly followed the others in.

Thump-thump.

"There they are!"

Otis headed briskly across the floor of a grand chamber lined floor to ceiling with books. A low table flanked by highback chairs stood at the head of the room, in front of a stone hearth where a fire blazed briskly.

Thump-thump. Thump-thump.

Sebastian's eyes widened as the apprehension suffusing his veins turned into full-blown revulsion.

Sitting next to the pile of journals belonging to Catherine Boone was a thin book covered with black leather and bearing a red metal clasp.

His gaze locked onto it unerringly. The room faded around him.

Sebastian's heart pounded rapidly in his chest, an untamed beat that chilled him to the bones and filled him with horror. Bile rose in his throat.

Artemus frowned when he spotted the slim tome.

"That's the poetry book Cunningham brought to the shop for me to look at."

"Sebastian?" Callie had stopped in her tracks. Anxious lines furrowed her brow as she turned and studied him. "Are you okay?"

His sister's voice reached him fuzzily, as if her words were travelling across a great distance. Heat spread through Sebastian. It seeped through his flesh and blood from his very core, a growing conflagration that would burn him to cinders. His marks tingled and throbbed.

He knew this sickening feeling.

No! Not here! Not now!

∾

ARTEMUS STARED. "WHAT THE—?"

Sebastian stood frozen behind them. Power flared in his eyes, a dazzling radiance that was echoed by the uncanny glow growing on his palms and the vest pocket where his watch sat. He was staring unblinkingly at the poetry book on the coffee table.

"What's wrong with him?" Peirce asked.

"I don't know," Artemus muttered.

He could feel the divine energy in Sebastian escalating exponentially.

Otis drew a sudden sharp breath. "Oh!"

Artemus looked at his assistant.

Otis's alarmed gaze shifted between the black leather tome and Sebastian. "It's resonating with him!"

Trepidation shot through Artemus at his words. As if to prove his assistant right, the book trembled before levitating off the table, the metal clasp and leather throbbing with a sinister black and crimson light.

The Vatican agents drew their weapons. The room started to shake violently around them.

"Uh-oh," Haruki muttered.

He morphed into his dragon form and released his blade.

"I think he's awakening!" Callie yelled above the noise of the books falling off the walls.

She shifted into the Chimera, her scepter in hand.

Artemus unleashed his own sword, his pulse racing. "Does that mean the book is his gate? But he said he'd hidden it!"

"It's the other half!" Drake exchanged an anxious glance with him, dark blade and shield at the ready and eyes glowing scarlet. "Remember? He only had part of his gate!"

"What's happening?" Peirce shouted.

Artemus clenched his jaw. There was no stopping what was taking place before them, however unfortunate their present circumstances were. "You're about to witness the awakening of a divine beast in the presence of his gate. Get ready."

"Why?" one of the Vatican agents said, ashen-faced.

"Because we're going to get a lot of uninvited guests," Artemus said grimly.

The air split open with a dozen booming claps. Crimson-tinged portals burst into existence above them.

Peirce replaced the magazine in his gun hurriedly. "Shit."

Sebastian's pocket watch was now in his left hand, the artifact a golden whip once more. Divine light shimmered along its length where it moved agitatedly, the lash behaving as if it were sentient.

Artemus's stomach plummeted when the tome of

poetry hurtled across the chamber, nearly catching Peirce and another agent in the back of the head. It stopped a couple of feet in front of Sebastian and spun upright until it faced him.

A sphere of light exploded into existence in Sebastian's right hand. He held it out to his side and released it. The ball ascended slowly into the air. It dropped suddenly, carving the very fabric of space and ripping apart a breach that pulsed with a golden light as it fell and vanished.

Sebastian's hands twitched. He blinked and moved his head with some difficulty, as if fighting a force greater than him.

"Stop me," he told Artemus between gritted teeth.

"What?"

"*I said stop me!*" Sebastian roared.

"But you're awakening, brother!" Callie said, her anguish plain to see.

"You do not understand!" The radiance faded briefly from Sebastian's eyes. Fear clouded his dark gaze. "This rift will lead them to the other half of my gate. You have to stop me. Even if you need to kill me!"

Smokey whined and pawed the ground.

Artemus frowned. "I think killing you would be taking things a bit—"

"Why, thank you," someone growled, interrupting him.

Artemus looked up and swore.

Cunningham floated some fifteen feet above them, his dark wings swatting the air lazily and his broadsword in hand. An army of demons was swarming out of the portals around him. Among them were a dozen of the monstrous, two-headed hellhounds Callie and Smokey had fought once before.

Artemus's knuckles whitened on the hilt of his blade.

The demon commander's earlier retreat had clearly given him time to gather reinforcements. He had never meant to abandon this battle.

Cunningham flashed a mocking smile at Artemus, as if he'd read his thoughts.

His gaze moved to Sebastian, his eyes turning ferocious in their intensity. "I think we should go check out this gate of yours, my dear earl."

Artemus's pulse jumped. His wings unfurled just as Cunningham dove.

Smokey snarled and leapt.

The demon commander snatched the black leather tome from the air, slammed into Sebastian, and carried him into the golden portal. Smokey's jaws closed on Cunningham's left ankle. The hellhound vanished inside the rift.

The demon army followed, their passage splitting the air with a deafening roar as they plunged swiftly after Cunningham.

"Not so fast, you bastards!" Artemus growled.

He beat his wings, clasped his sword in a double-handed grip, and launched himself headlong into the breach, the others following in his wake.

CHAPTER THIRTY-SIX

WARM LIGHT DANCED AROUND SEBASTIAN, A kaleidoscope of dazzling golds and whites. He was dimly aware of Cunningham's weight pressing on his chest as they hurtled through the rift, a swarm of demons on their heels. Surprise shot through him when he caught a glimpse of the demon commander's face.

Cunningham was gnashing his teeth, as if he were in pain. So too were the fiends following him, some even groaning and whimpering.

Is it because this rift is different?

Sebastian gasped as they abruptly exited the portal. Gravity took over.

There was no more time to think.

He fell through empty air for a timeless moment. Pain exploded across his back as he crashed onto a marble floor, fracturing dozens of cracks into it. Numbness shot down his legs. His beast raged behind his eyes.

"Where is it?" Cunningham snarled.

The demon landed next to Sebastian, grabbed him by the front of his vest, and lifted him off the ground. He shook him violently before slamming him back down again with vicious force.

Stars burst across Sebastian's vision as his skull connected sharply with the checkered marble.

"Where is your gate?!" Cunningham roared.

Motion above the demon drew Sebastian's dazed gaze. A shadow was moving rapidly toward them, its shape blurring as it sprung from one marble pillar to another, using the columns lining the galleries to control its fall.

Smokey landed on the demon's back and knocked him off Sebastian.

Sebastian panted as he rose slowly on his elbows, his head and back throbbing, the stickiness of hot blood coating the back of his scalp.

Smokey shook himself and morphed into Cerberus where he stood facing Cunningham, his golden eyes glowing with hate and a continuous growl rumbling out of his throats. The demon army descended around them.

Thump-thump.

Sebastian's gaze found the black leather tome where it lay a few feet to his left. He winced as he scrambled onto his hands and knees. He rose unsteadily, desperation lending him a burst of strength.

I have to get rid of it!

Smokey's voice reached him then.

Go, brother! Our brethren are almost here. I will hold the demons back until they arrive!

Sebastian's eyes met the hellhound's.

"Thank you, brother," he whispered.

Heat singed his skin as he grabbed the poetry book off the floor. He bolted for the birdcage elevator in the corner of the atrium, heart pounding. The lion and the eagle on his palms were growing alarmingly hot. And the itching

between his shoulder blades and at his tailbone had started
anew.

COOL AIR SLAMMED INTO ARTEMUS WHEN HE SHOT OUT
the other side of the golden rift.

An immense space spanning seven stories appeared
beneath him. His eyes widened as he started to fall again.

"This looks familiar!" Drake shouted, plummeting
beside him.

"Where the hell are we?!" Callie yelled, arms
pinwheeling wildly to Artemus's left.

Artemus got a glimpse of ornate iron balconies and
galleries of bookcases. "Well, I'll be damned! We're in
Salem!"

"Salem, Wales?!" Peirce said.

"More like Massachusetts!" Haruki said.

Serena scowled at Artemus and Drake as she and Nate
plunged past them. "Now that we've all had a nice chit
chat, how about you two haul ass and save us before we
crash into the floor of Sebastian's library like bugs on a
windshield?!"

Artemus and Drake spread their wings and darted
through the air in blistering-fast moves, grabbing raining
bodies and casting them unceremoniously into the
galleries they passed.

Smokey's voice reached Artemus. *Hurry!*

He caught sight of the three-headed hellhound where
the latter stood fighting a horde of demons and hellbeasts
below them. Of Cunningham and Sebastian there was no
sign. Anger filled Artemus when he saw the bloodied
gashes on Smokey's flanks.

"Shit!"

He followed Drake's alarmed gaze.

Peirce and Otis were fifteen feet from the ground and the roiling mass of demons.

Artemus and Drake folded their wings and dove.

Smokey leapt from the crowd of fiends at the last second and broke the two men's fall. The demon horde and beasts regrouped around them, obsidian eyes flaring with hunger. They fell back with angry shrieks as Artemus and Drake landed heavily in their midst.

Artemus swung his blade and cleaved the head off a demon. "Hands off my damn hound!"

"Hey, he's my hound too," Drake protested.

"Alright, hands off *our* hound."

Artemus narrowed his eyes and pointed his blade threateningly at a double-headed hellbeast. The monster squinted at the sword, snatched it in its jaws, and flung the weapon and Artemus clean across the atrium.

Artemus swore. He crashed into Haruki just as the latter dropped from the fifth gallery. They landed in a tangle of limbs, wings, and tail, and slid across the marble floor before fetching up against a wall.

"Ouch," the Colchian Dragon mumbled beneath him.

Callie lowered herself beside them, her snake tail unwinding from the spindle of an ornate railing. "I know you haven't had any alone time lately, but this is really not the place to be getting amorous, guys."

"Yeah, keep it in your pants, you two," Serena muttered, landing in a low crouch next to Callie.

Nate thudded down beside them.

Artemus climbed onto his hands and knees. "For the last time, Haruki and I don't have that kind of relationship!"

The Colchian Dragon sighed. "That would be more convincing if you weren't touching my groin right now."

Drake glared at them from where he, Smokey, Peirce, and Otis stood surrounded by dozens of demons. "Will you clowns get with the program?!"

CHAPTER THIRTY-SEVEN

SEBASTIAN EXITED THE ELEVATOR AND RACED ACROSS THE shadowy basement. An orange glow pierced the gloom up ahead. He headed toward it, blood thrumming in his veins.

A corrupt, black cloud pulsing with scarlet light had engulfed the poetry book in his hand. He gritted his teeth as it stung his flesh.

I have to get to the boiler room!

The air ripped behind him just as he reached the door. Sebastian spun around.

Cunningham stepped out of the scarlet rift that had appeared in the library's basement. "There you are."

Sebastian drew a sphere of divine light and cast it angrily at the demon commander.

Cunningham twisted out of the way with a flick of his wings. He watched the globe smash a crater into the wall behind him before gazing mockingly at Sebastian, his crimson eyes flaring with hate.

"Your aim is terrible."

The demon folded his wings and shot straight at Sebastian, closing the distance between them in the blink of an eye.

A grunt of pain left Sebastian as they slammed into the boiler room door. Searing pain pierced his body in the next instant, robbing him of breath. His grip slackened on his whip.

"What is in there, little boy?" Cunningham hissed in Sebastian's ear.

Sebastian choked on a mouthful of blood.

Cunningham's broadsword was embedded in his chest and had carved straight through his back and into the door behind, pinning him in place.

Agony filled Sebastian's world. He bit his lip and held back the scream bubbling up his throat. He was dimly aware of his beast pacing to and fro deep inside his soul, the creature's frustration so thick it was almost palpable.

A surprised sound left Cunningham as he stared through the narrow glass window at the top of the boiler room door. "What is that?"

That was when Sebastian's beast spoke to him.

It is time, child.

Sebastian stiffened as he glimpsed the form of the creature who lived within him. It was moving out of the shadows it usually dwelled in, its shape becoming more distinct.

It is time for us to fully awaken.

Horror washed through Sebastian.

"No," he mumbled weakly.

Cunningham gave him a puzzled look before reaching for the deadbolts on the door.

Sebastian's beast stilled, anger emanating from him in a thick, cold surge.

I saved you once before from this demon, child. The night I first started to awaken. It was never meant to be. For it was your descendant who was fated to bear the soul of a divine beast.

Shock blasted through Sebastian.

But I chose you instead. Not only because you were at death's door and I would have had to find another human bloodline to form a contract with. But because you were worthy. Even as a child, yours was a pure and bright spirit. One whose strength was equal to that of Heaven's most powerful warriors. I chose you to bear my sacred bond and to be my ally. So, I will ask you this, child. Do you want power? The power to kill this demon? The power to erase the existence of the abominable creature who slayed your family?

A flood of emotion stormed Sebastian as his beast's words echoed inside his skull. This was the most the creature had ever said to him in the lifetime they had known one another.

His parents and sisters' faces swam before him.

Cunningham cursed as the iron bars burned his demon skin. Nanorobots burst forth from his flesh and wrapped around the deadbolts. The metal locks moved.

Sebastian's beast spoke once more, his voice growing more forceful.

Speak, child! And tell me this. Do you wish to claim your rightful place among your brethren? They who are putting their lives on the line and fighting for you this very moment in time?!

Sebastian closed his eyes, a wave of lassitude washing over him. He could sense the others' energies above him as they battled Cunningham's demon army. He pictured his newfound sister and his brother. Artemus and Drake. Haruki and Otis. Serena and Nate. He thought of the connections that had been forged between them in the short time they had known each other. Bonds he could not deny. An alliance he would not betray. A divine destiny he could no longer refuse.

He drew a shaky breath and whispered, "Yes."

The beast's satisfaction resonated loudly through him, warming his chilled flesh.

Good. Hold on to the whip and the book.

Sebastian could feel the heat of the fire inside the boiler room through the window behind his head. It grew exponentially as Cunningham pushed open the heavy, metal door, taking him with it.

Cunningham stepped inside the chamber. He paused and stared.

"What have you done?" the demon commander growled.

Sebastian opened his eyes and raised his head. A savage smile curled his bloodied lips as he gazed at the closely guarded secret he had kept and defended from demons for ten years.

"That is a cauldron of molten iron. If you want the other half of my gate, you will have to remove it from the bottom."

Rage darkened the demon's face as he glared at the black pot sitting atop a blazing, fire-brick forge. He flew above the furnace and stared into the vessel of boiling metal, heedless of the immense heat roiling off it.

Prepare yourself.

A burst of divine force rushed through Sebastian's veins from the beast, energizing him.

Cunningham clenched his jaw, grabbed the edges of the cauldron, and pushed, the muscles in his arms bunching under the weight of the iron within.

Sebastian's eyes widened.

The stink of burning flesh filled the boiler room as the

pot started to tip over. The demon bared his teeth, his eyes blazing a bright vermillion. He roared and gave the cauldron a final shove.

A river of glowing metal spilled onto the floor of the boiler room as it came crashing down. Some of it splashed onto the demon, scorching dark wounds in his body.

Cunningham ignored the injuries, his hateful gaze locked on the artifact revealed in the middle of the cooling pool of iron. He reached down and picked it up, the metal coating it charring his fingers.

It was a slim tome covered in red leather, with a black metal clasp.

Cunningham looked triumphantly at Sebastian. "I win."

Thump.

A dark cloud burst forth around the book of poetry in the demon's hold. It writhed and pulsed in tandem with the shadow-wreathed tome in Sebastian's hand.

Thump-thump.

Sebastian's heart echoed the evil crimson light beating at the core of the two objects. His breath stilled as the red book levitated sharply out of Cunningham's grasp. The black tome was wrenched from his own grip by the same invisible force a second later.

The books ascended into midair.

A ferocious grimace distorted Cunningham's face.

Waves of evil energy rippled around the chamber as the two pieces of the artifact started merging into one.

The marks on Sebastian's hands grew hotter.

Thump-thump. Thump-thump.

Silver light flared on the golden whip in his right hand. Symbols appeared along the lash's smooth length. Sebastian stared, transfixed.

He recognized the ancient words.

They were written in the same Enochian language he had unearthed in some of the rare books in his possession —the same language that Catherine Boone had used to pen her journals.

A voice left Sebastian's throat in a deep rumble. It was not his own.

He gritted his teeth and grasped the handle of the demon broadsword lodged in his body as his beast started translating the holy sigils. Power flared inside him as he slowly removed the blade from his flesh. His wound sealed in seconds, the edges glowing briefly with divine light.

Up ahead, the two books had fused fully and now formed a rectangle of rapidly expanding blackness.

"*Yes!*" Cunningham hissed, his attention focused on the gate.

The first symbol on Sebastian's whip flashed gold. It turned crimson with his next heartbeat.

The room started to shake. Grains of plaster and dirt rained down upon them.

The gate throbbed and swelled, evil incarnate.

Cunningham looked at the quaking ceiling. He raised his hands in a welcoming gesture, his crimson eyes glowing with glee.

"*Come, my brothers and sisters!*" the demon commander bellowed. "*Join me! Our time is finally here!*"

Sebastian knew Cunningham was addressing more than just the creatures in the library above them. His ears popped as the pressure inside the room dropped abruptly.

Darkness was gathering above them. Hell was coming to Salem.

The whip trembled in Sebastian's grip as more symbols flashed gold then red.

Fire bloomed inside his soul. The marks on his palms flashed with brightness. The itching at the base of his spine became a growth that lengthened rapidly. His shoulder blades quivered and sprouted out from his back, the muscles and bones unravelling before knitting back together into something new. Something different.

The last incantation left Sebastian's lips.

The whip thickened and sprouted two more cords from its handle, an incandescent radiance throbbing along the three lashes as the weapon adopted its true form.

A divine explosion detonated inside Sebastian, so fierce and glorious it rendered him blind and deaf for an instant. His beast growled as their souls finally merged, the sound full of joy and gratification.

The brightness faded. Awareness returned.

Sebastian opened his eyes, the name of the creature bonded to him echoing through his very being. A feral smile curved his mouth as he looked upon the demon before him.

CHAPTER THIRTY-EIGHT

ARTEMUS PIVOTED IN MIDAIR, HIS BROADSWORD SLICING two winged demons in half. Drake appeared beside him as the creatures plummeted toward the ground, black blood spurting briefly from their carved-up bodies before they turned to ash.

Artemus observed the battlefield below with narrowed eyes. "Is it me or are these bastards getting a bit sluggish?"

"It's the iron." Drake indicated the ornate balconies lining the floors of the underground library. "This place is full of it. It's dulling their senses. And holding my own demon at bay." He grimaced. "I hate to admit it, but that guy is one twisted genius."

A flood of dark energy blasted through the atrium, rattling the crystal chandelier above them and toppling books from the cases in the galleries. The demon horde roared as the evil force filled them with renewed strength, their obsidian eyes flaring brightly with power.

"Shit," Drake muttered.

Artemus's hands clenched on the hilt of his broadsword.

The wave had originated from beneath the library. Black lines ripped the space around them asunder.

Artemus gritted his teeth when he saw the army of demons approaching through the pulsing, crimson rifts.

"The gate's opening!" Drake yelled.

An explosion ripped through the floor below them, scattering demons and Vatican agents alike. Fragments of marble and plaster fountained into the air.

Two figures shot up out of the gaping, dark space beneath the library and ascended rapidly toward the ceiling, along with a doorway of throbbing blackness.

Artemus's eyes rounded as they climbed past him and Drake.

DRAKE GAZED UNBLINKINGLY AT THE CREATURE AND the demon locked in battle some fifteen feet above them.

The divine beast frowned at his opponent, the powerful eagle wings on his back thumping the air with effortless grace as he hovered in the air. A large snake protruded from the base of his spine, the serpent's eyes aglow with the same white light that brightened its host's dazzling gaze.

In the beast's right hand was a mass of divine energy in the shape of a roaring lion's head. It was directed at the immense gate behind the creature and was slowly sucking the darkness out of it, much to the horror of the demon commander who faced him.

In the beast's left hand, the lashes dancing through the air as if they were alive, was an intricate, golden, triple-thronged whip that glowed with a holy light.

Cunningham growled and lunged toward the divine beast.

Sebastian bared his teeth and cracked the whip, the cords carving the air with a sound like thunder. The lashes burned dark lines into the demon's body, forcing him to retreat.

"Wow," Artemus murmured.

Drake glanced at his brother. "Do you know the name of his beast?"

"You mean you don't?"

Drake frowned. "No, wise ass."

Artemus grinned and cocked a thumb at Sebastian. "That's the Sphinx. I kinda suspected that's who he was from the marks on his hands and his connection to Callie and Smokey, but I wasn't sure until now."

Demons surged out of the rifts and barreled toward Sebastian and Hell's gate, their yellow eyes aglow with determination.

Artemus dropped his blade casually on his shoulder, beat his wings, and rose. "Let's go help our new friend, shall we?"

"Show off," Drake muttered as he followed in his twin's wake.

～

"HEY, WATCH THE TAILS!" SERENA SNAPPED.

"Sorry!" Haruki and Callie shouted.

Smokey growled out an apology.

Serena offered her hand to Peirce and hauled him off the floor.

"Thank you." The Vatican group leader turned and studied the Colchian Dragon and the Chimera. "Are they always so...excitable during battle?"

Serena sighed. Haruki and Callie were smiling savagely as they slayed the fiends around them, weapons and faces dripping with dark demon blood and eyes fairly blazing with delight. Smokey was similarly enjoying himself where he batted away at the fiends with his giant paws and ripped into their throats with frenzied snarls.

"Yeah, well, they kinda hate demons. It's in their blood."

"Elton was right," Peirce mumbled.

"Why? What did he say?"

Nate strode over and handed her an EMP device. "We're going to need this."

Serena followed his gaze to the figures with liquid-silver eyes descending toward them. A grimace twisted her lips. "Great. Now we have winged super soldier demons. This day just keeps getting better."

Movement behind Nate drew her gaze.

Serena scowled and reached for his shoulder. "Watch out!"

CALLIE GRIPPED HER SCEPTER, TWISTED ON HER HEELS, and flung it at the two-headed hellhound springing toward Nate. The weapon skewered the monster and brought it to the floor. She strode to where it lay pinned and writhing on the ground, took hold of the golden staff, and ripped it out of its body before roaring out a jet of fire.

Divine flames engulfed the demon beast. Its screams faded as it burst into a heavy cloud of ash.

"Stay away from my boyfriend, hellhound!" the Chimera hissed at the pile of cinders.

"What?" Serena stared from Callie to Nate and back. "You guys are dating? Since when?!"

"Oh." An embarrassed expression dawned on Callie's face. She scratched her head distractedly, the golden serpents that made up her mane coiling around her fingers with loving hisses. "I guess we forgot to tell you, huh?"

"It was when we broke into Cunningham's house," Haruki explained helpfully before disposing of two demons. He swatted a third into a wall with his tail and grinned. "She also specified there would be no intercourse before their third date."

Several Vatican agents turned and stared at a blushing Callie. Nate's ears reddened.

SWEAT BROKE OUT ACROSS SEBASTIAN'S BROW AS HE poured more power into the lion-shaped sphere. The gate was starting to close, the darkness wreathing it growing dimmer. Enraged shrieks reverberated around him as the demons in their midst expressed their resentment.

"How much longer?!" Artemus shouted to Sebastian's left.

He dove beneath a flurry of talons, thrust his blade through the throat of a winged demon, and beheaded two more, his movements so swift his body blurred.

Drake flashed through the air on the other side of Sebastian, a deadly shadow that felled as many demons as appeared in his path.

Cunningham had temporarily retreated from the fight, his gaze blazing with hate as he observed them from above.

No doubt coming up with another plan, the devious snake.

Sebastian clenched his jaw. He would not let the demon win. Nor would he let down the companions who were fighting beside him. His beast growled in agreement.

"It is almost done."

OTIS STARED, MESMERIZED, AT THE BATTLE UNFOLDING around him.

He was near the south wall of the atrium, the defensive barrier that had protected him from the demons in Cunningham's castle still in effect and holding back the creatures that sought to tear him to pieces.

Though he had heard details of the battles in New York and in L.A., it was his first time witnessing the divine beasts, the angels, and their super soldier and human allies in a full-fledged, all-out clash with so many demons. It was also his first time seeing a gate to Hell.

The fear that had been his constant companion since Cunningham first appeared before him a handful of days past should have had him on his knees in terror. But it didn't.

All Otis felt was an eerie sense of calm as he gazed at the doorway of throbbing darkness in the air above him.

It was as if he already knew what was about to happen. As if everything taking place before him had been preordained. Knowledge filled him, along with a heat that originated from the very core of his being.

In that moment, the world had never looked clearer to Otis.

He knew what he needed to do next.

CHAPTER THIRTY-NINE

OUR BROTHER IS QUITE SOMETHING TO BEHOLD.

Callie glanced at Smokey before studying Sebastian where the latter manipulated the leonine lightning ball that was shutting down his gate, his eagle wings striking the air with strong thumps to keep him afloat and his golden whip slicing through the odd demon that managed to get past his angelic guard.

"He is that," she muttered. "By the way, am I the only one suddenly remembering how he used to chase us around the place with those light spheres of his?"

No. Smokey huffed out a sigh. *Those things stung.*

The air shivered with a sudden flood of energy.

Callie froze at the formidable divine force that had just blasted across the library. The snakes on her head and the one making up her tail stilled and turned as one.

Smokey straightened to his full height beside her, his three-headed gaze locking on the figure near the south wall of the atrium. Haruki appeared on the other side of him, his Dragon eyes widening with the same wonderment rising inside her and the hellhound.

A hush descended around them, even the demons pausing at what they had just discerned in their midst.

"Is that coming from Otis?" Serena said quietly behind Callie.

Callie dipped her chin and swallowed, in awe of the incredible presence she was sensing. "Yes."

~

FIRE ERUPTED ON OTIS'S FOREHEAD AND IN HIS RIGHT palm. He gazed down at his hand and was only mildly surprised when he saw the mark that appeared in blazing, white light at the base of his middle finger.

The conflagration burning up his soul intensified. He felt something sprout from his back. Then, he was rising.

~

SEBASTIAN GRUNTED AS THE GATE TO HELL FINALLY closed, the booming clap echoed by the screams of the thousands of invisible fiends trapped behind it. The demons around them faltered, the blaze fading from their eyes.

The two books of poetry slowly resumed their original forms. Sebastian snatched them from the air as they started to fall, his pulse racing with elation.

Oh.

He blinked at his beast's surprise. Then, he felt it. The life force that had brought everyone around and below him to a standstill.

He had been so focused on his task he had only dimly registered its existence.

"Otis," Artemus breathed where he hovered next to Sebastian.

Drake joined them and watched the figure ascend from the atrium, his face filled with astonishment.

Otis's pale wings shimmered with divine energy, the feathers barely flickering as he climbed. Yet, every gentle beat generated enough force to make the air tremble and thump painfully against Sebastian's eardrums.

A third eye had appeared on the young man's forehead. It burned with a dazzling light. The same light that was pulsing from his right hand. His skin had taken on a silver sheen very much like Artemus's and golden armor encased his body from the neck down. His dark hair had brightened to the color of the sun.

The seraph stopped in front of them. His wise eyes locked on Sebastian. He smiled faintly and extended a hand wordlessly toward him.

Give him the tomes.

Sebastian blinked at his beast's reverential tone.

On the floor of the atrium, Callie, Haruki, and Smokey were crouched down on one knee, their posture one of deference as their beasts bowed their heads to the seraph. Even Artemus and Drake had lowered their blades.

Sebastian hesitated, heart pounding. He passed the two halves of his gate reluctantly to the angel.

He could not disobey his beast. Nor could he refuse the command of the being before him.

"*No!*" Cunningham roared.

He plunged past the demons escaping into the rifts around him, his shape blurring as he aimed for Otis.

Sebastian rose to intercept him, the triple-thronged whip flaring with power in his grasp. He smashed shoulder first into the demon and carried him toward one of the pillars spanning a balcony.

Marble exploded around them as they smashed into the column. Sebastian closed a hand around Cunningham's throat, the golden lashes of his whip twisting around the demon's body and trapping his wings and arms.

Cunningham growled and fought the ties binding him, his eyes burning with loathing. With Serena and Nate having activated their EMP devices, no nanorobots would be coming to his aid this time around.

Sebastian looked over his shoulder to where Otis floated, his expression still serene. "Go ahead. I have him."

The seraph dipped his chin slightly. The two books rose from his grasp and spun upright until they faced him. His mouth opened.

The holy incantation he whispered made the chamber vibrate and rattled Sebastian's very bones, the ancient, sacred words leaving his lips in a melody that could have scorched the very Earth.

A radiant beam in the shape of an inverted V exploded from Otis's right hand and struck the books. The artifacts trembled as they were engulfed by pure divine essence. Then they were crumbling, their matter turning to gold dust that dropped into the seraph's grasp.

Otis closed his fingers around the glowing remains of Hell's gate. His third eye flared. He opened his hand.

His palm was empty.

"*Damn you!*" Cunningham screamed, spit bursting from his mouth.

He shifted into his human form, slipped out of Sebastian's grasp and the clutches of the whip, and leapt toward the last rift as it started to close.

Sebastian turned, his body heating up with a burst of power. He flapped his wings and cracked his whip.

The triple cords extended to three times their length and closed around Cunningham's right leg. The demon shrieked as the thongs tightened, cleaving his limb clean off.

"That is for my mother," Sebastian growled.

He snapped the weapon again. The lashes sliced through the demon's left leg at the knee as he started to fall toward the shrinking portal.

"That is for my father." Sebastian spun the whip above his head, pale tails of energy trailing from the ends of the lashes. "This is for my sisters."

Black blood exploded from Cunningham's arms as the weapon sheared his limbs from his trunk. Sebastian dove and grabbed the demon by the neck, halting his descent.

"And this?" he hissed icily as he gazed into the fiend's loathsome eyes, "*this* is for me."

Blinding light exploded inside Sebastian's right hand and engulfed the demon's throat. Cunningham screamed.

His voice faded as the divine sphere ripped through his flesh and turned it to ash.

Sebastian released the disintegrating corpse and watched it fall inside the rift. The portal closed with a shearing sound.

Deafening silence echoed in its wake.

Something fell past Sebastian.

Artemus flashed through the air and caught Otis just before he hit the floor of the atrium. Sebastian and Drake followed swiftly. The others gathered hurriedly around them as Artemus carefully laid the unconscious man on the ground.

Otis was back in his human form, the third eye fading fast from the center of his forehead.

"What on earth just happened?" Peirce said, ashen-faced, as he gripped a broken arm.

"Is he okay?" Serena asked tensely.

"Yeah." Artemus blew out a sigh of relief as he lifted his fingers from the pulse beating at the base of Otis's throat. "He just fainted."

They stared at the motionless man.

A timid voice reached them from a distance in the ensuing hush.

"Er, excuse me?"

They looked up.

A face was peering over the edge of what remained of the giant crystal chandelier suspended from the library's ceiling.

"Could someone give me a hand?" the Vatican agent called out.

Peirce stared. "How long have you been up there?"

The Vatican agent grimaced. "Since we came out of the rift. I wanted to shout for help, but you guys looked busy."

CHAPTER FORTY

"OTIS DID WHAT?" ELTON ASKED LEADENLY.

"He destroyed a gate to Hell," Artemus repeated.

He glanced at the inert man lying on his living room couch. It was four in the morning and they were back in Chicago.

Otis's chest rose and fell shallowly as he slept, a blanket atop him. He had still not regained consciousness since the aftermath of the battle in Salem.

Having refused Sebastian's offer of passage to England through a rift, Peirce and his agents were on a flight back to London.

"No offence, but I don't think I'm going to get used to that mode of travel anytime soon," Peirce had said with a grimace as they stood outside Sebastian's bookstore.

With Sebastian's jet still in England and the rest of them similarly unkeen to take a trip through a portal, they had flown to Chicago on Callie's private plane. Artemus had roused Elton when they'd landed at the airport. His old friend and mentor had been waiting for them on the porch when they pulled up the mansion's driveway, his clothes and hair in mild disarray.

Artemus suspected Helen had been at his place when he'd called him.

Elton looked blindly at Otis. "That's impossible! The Vatican have extensively tested their structural integrity. They didn't manage to put a single dent in Callie and Haruki's gates!"

"Well, Otis did," Sebastian murmured. "We all saw it."

Callie, Haruki, and Drake glanced uneasily at each other where they stood and sat around the lounge. They could all still feel an echo of power from the seraph who had come to life before them.

Nate walked into the room with a tray of coffee and sandwiches, Serena and Smokey in his wake. The rabbit was munching hungrily on a mouthful of freshly fried bacon where he perched in Serena's arms.

"Thank you," Elton muttered to Nate when the latter offered him a cup. A thoughtful frown wrinkled his brow as he looked at Artemus. "Do you have any idea what Otis is?"

Artemus hesitated before shaking his head, troubled. "I don't, I'm afraid."

"Something tells me he does, though," Serena said.

She was gazing at Sebastian. The rest of them turned and stared.

Sebastian stiffened, a defensive light dawning in his eyes. "I have my suspicions, but I am not completely confident about my deductions."

"Just spit it out, will you?" Drake said testily.

Sebastian shifted uneasily under their gazes.

"This is only a theory, but from the third eye that

appeared on his forehead and the mark on his palm, I believe him to be the Seal," he said reluctantly.

"The Seal?" Callie repeated, mystified. "The Seal of what?"

Sebastian glanced at his sister, his expression grave. "The Seal of God."

Stunned silence fell around them.

A muscle jumped in Drake's cheek. "Do you mean one of the Seven Seals?"

Serena frowned. "What are those?"

"The Seven Seals are mentioned in the Book of Revelation," Sebastian told the super soldier. "They protect a document that is said to herald the End of Days." He met Drake's tense stare. "The answer to your question is no. I do not believe he is one of the Seven Seals." He paused. "Do you recall when he spoke?"

Callie shuddered. "Yes. His voice was—"

"—so potent, it could have crushed cities," Haruki muttered.

Sebastian nodded solemnly. "Indeed. The Seal of God was also said to be the Voice of God."

Elton blanched. "Wait. Do you mean—?"

"Metatron?" Drake said, pale-faced.

"Yes," Sebastian said. "That is one of the names attributed to him. Although the Books of Enoch refer to Uriel as the first Archangel, there was one before him. The only seraph who was allowed to sit in the presence of God. The Primordial Angel."

Otis mumbled in his sleep and shifted slightly under the blanket. They all stared at him.

"Wow," Haruki mumbled. "Metatron is an antique shop owner's assistant?"

Artemus narrowed his eyes at the Colchian Dragon

before turning to Sebastian. "I've been meaning to ask you something. The rift you opened to Salem. Why was it different from the one you created in London?"

Sebastian grimaced and rubbed the back of his head. "I believe the London portal was a passage through the same dimension where Hell exists. I used the remnants of the one Cunningham had created to reproduce it."

Artemus shuddered as he recalled the gruesome scenes they had witnessed during their short passage through the crimson rift. "And the second portal?"

Sebastian faltered. "My best guess is that *that* one was a...Heavenly gate. Cunningham and the demons seemed to be in pain when we were travelling through it, as if the light was physically hurting them."

The color had drained from Elton's face.

"There's still a lot I don't get." Serena fisted her hand and stared at her clenched fingers. "Besides the fact that we still don't know how Ba'al managed to incorporate super soldier technology inside the bodies of demons, what happened when Cunningham stabbed me with his artificial blade is something I've never experienced before." She looked up at them, her eyes full of unease. "He disabled my nanorobots and my ability to self-heal. I was bleeding pretty heavily before you guys appeared on that tower."

"What?" Nate said, shocked.

"You never said anything," Drake said, his tone accusing.

Serena made a face. "We haven't exactly had time for a debrief."

Artemus frowned. "How come you were still standing and fighting when we got there?"

Serena looked over at Otis. "He fixed me and reactivated my nanorobots."

Otis mumbled again and moved on the couch.

"That's pretty amazing," Haruki blurted out in an awed tone.

Artemus swallowed. He could only guess at the amount of divine energy Otis must have used to achieve that feat in so short a time.

"The demon commander you killed," Elton said to Sebastian. "His name was Amaymon?"

Sebastian nodded, a muscle jumping in his jawline. "Yes. Amaymon was a Prince of Hell said to possess a poisonous breath. He is the one who awakened inside Cunningham, broke into my estate, and slaughtered my family."

Elton digested this information with a perturbed look before turning to Artemus and Drake. "You said you met your mother? In separate visions?"

Artemus and Drake exchanged a cautious glance.

"Yes," Drake said. "Although we've both since realized they weren't just visions."

"It sure as hell didn't feel like one," Serena muttered.

Elton gazed warily at the super soldier. Serena had told them how she and Otis had bound Samyaza in the depths of Drake's soul. From Elton's expression, he still considered that story somewhat far-fetched.

Although the identity of Drake's demon had initially come as a shock to Artemus too, he realized it should not truly have surprised him.

"Has the Vatican discovered anything in Oxford or London that might help us figure out Ba'al's next move?" he asked Elton.

Elton shook his head. "No." He glanced at Haruki.

"But the Sigil of Baphomet trick means we can hopefully start to identify more of their meeting places."

The Yakuza heir smiled. "Ogawa is a hard task master when it comes to card games."

Otis gasped and bolted upright on the couch, startling them all. He grabbed the blanket at his waist in a white-knuckled grip and looked around wildly. "Where—where are we? What happened?" He swallowed nervously as he met Artemus's eyes. "Where are the demons?!"

Callie clutched her chest. "Jesus, you almost gave us a heart attack!"

"Heart attack?" Haruki muttered. "I nearly soiled my underpants."

"Sorry," Otis mumbled.

He pulled the blanket off and slowly swung his legs over the edge of the couch, his face pale.

Haruki observed him with a pensive frown before looking over at Sebastian. "Are you sure about the Seal thing? Because all I'm getting from him right now is his usual geeky, dweeb vibe."

"Do you remember what happened?" Artemus asked Otis tensely.

"I—" Otis faltered. "I...don't know."

"The third eye? The angel wings? The crazy powerful voice? The light show?" Serena raised an eyebrow. "Any of this ringing bells?"

Otis's fingers trembled as he raised a hand to his forehead. He stared at his right palm. "Wait! That...that *really* happened?! I thought I dreamt it all!"

"No, it happened alright," Callie said emphatically.

There were nods all around.

"Would you like a sandwich?" Nate asked Otis.

Otis blinked. "Yes. Thank you."

Artemus pointed at Sebastian's watch where the chain hung out of his vest pocket. "By the way, can you tell us what that is?"

"Oh."

Sebastian removed the artifact. His eyes flashed with power. The watch morphed into the golden, three-lashed whip.

Elton stared.

Otis swallowed the mouthful of sandwich he'd just bitten into, adjusted his glasses, and squinted at the weapon. "That would be the Triple-Thronged Whip of Raguel."

Artemus raised an eyebrow. "Who's Raguel?"

Sebastian appeared somewhat stunned as he gazed at the whip. "He was known as the Angel of Justice and the Glorifier of God." Lines wrinkled his brow as he looked at Artemus. "Your knowledge of the bible is quite appalling. We should rectify that."

"No, thanks."

CHAPTER FORTY-ONE

SEBASTIAN INSPECTED THE MONSTROUS MACHINE BEFORE him for a full minute. He cursed under his breath, rummaged through the kitchen cabinets until he found what he was looking for, and wandered over to the cast-iron range.

Nate strolled inside the room a short while later, his hair still wet from his shower. He froze in his tracks. "Er. Hello."

"Good morning."

Sebastian greeted the super soldier with a polite nod.

Nate glanced out of the kitchen windows. Dawn was only just breaking across Chicago. His gaze moved to the old-fashioned, black enamel pot sitting on one of the range's hobs. Steam curled up from the spout, along with the smell of freshly brewed coffee.

Nate indicated the streamlined apparatus sitting atop the counter. "Do you want me to show you how to use the coffee machine?"

"I would appreciate that, thank you. It has all the appearances of a Gordian knot."

Nate stared.

Sebastian sighed. "A Gordian knot is—"

"I know what a Gordian knot is," Nate rumbled.

Sebastian poured himself a cup of black coffee and watched as Nate got an armful of ingredients out of the pantry and refrigerator.

"Do you always get up this early to make breakfast?"

"Super soldiers do not require much sleep." Nate cracked eggs in a mixing bowl, added flour, milk, and sugar, and placed the whole thing under the professional mixer next to the coffee machine. "Besides, I enjoy cooking. It relaxes me."

Sebastian took a sip of his drink and opened the newspaper on the table. "I guess I should inform you of my food preferences then."

Nate stiffened where he was laying dozens of bacon strips on a tray. He turned and gazed wordlessly at Sebastian.

Serena walked in wearing her pajamas. She stopped abruptly when she spotted Sebastian at the kitchen table. "What the hell are you doing here?"

Sebastian sniffed. "Good morning to you too."

"I think he moved in," Nate told Serena.

Serena gave Sebastian a wary look. "Does Goldilocks know?"

Sebastian carefully avoided her gaze and adjusted his vest and cravat. "I am not sure why you are acting so surprised. Strictly speaking, I moved in two weeks ago."

Serena blinked. "You went home five days ago!"

"That was only to organize my personal affairs," Sebastian said coolly.

Drake wandered into the room in sweatpants and a T-shirt, Haruki following sluggishly behind him.

"You guys are up early," Serena said.

She took a cup out of the cabinet, placed it under the coffee machine, and punched a button.

"I think I'm still jetlagged," Drake grumbled.

Haruki narrowed his eyes at Nate. "And *I* hardly got any sleep last night."

Drake froze. He gaped at Sebastian. "What the hell is he doing here?!"

The coffee machine beeped.

Serena removed her cup and took a seat at the table. "Apparently, he lives here now."

Drake paled. "Does Artemus know?"

"I guess we'll find out soon enough," Serena murmured.

Footsteps sounded in the corridor leading off the kitchen. Everyone tensed.

Callie ambled in dressed in a beautiful, white, silk kimono gown decorated with dozens of koi fish. She padded barefoot to the kitchen range, rose on her tip toes, and kissed Nate.

Drake and Serena sucked in air. Sebastian's eyes widened.

Haruki frowned at the couple as he headed over to the coffee machine and started making himself a drink. "What happened to no sex before the third date?"

"Oh." Drake made a face. "Is that why you couldn't sleep?"

"Yeah," Haruki muttered. "My beast even forced me to wear ear plugs. I ended up coming down to the TV room and watching old soap reruns."

Callie ignored the chilly exchange and smiled at them beatifically. "I changed my mind. Besides, Oxford kind of counted as our first date and London our second. If you consider our trip to—*what the hell is he doing here?!*"

She gripped the neckline of her kimono and lifted an accusing finger at Sebastian.

"I live here." Sebastian frowned. "I must say that I do not approve of a young lady publicizing her relationship so openly, especially one to whom I am related." He glanced at Nate. "Even though I know Nathaniel to be a man of good standing, I must still protest, sister. There should be a proper period of courtship, followed by marriage, before you engage in such intimate acts."

There was a collective dropping of jaws around the kitchen.

Callie scowled. "Wait a goddamn minute! Are you saying you're gonna stop me sleeping with Nate just because you're my older brother?!"

"I am aware neither of you are novices when it comes to affairs of the flesh, but yes, I must insist, if only for the sake of your reputation," Sebastian said stiffly.

"To be honest, I kinda thought Nate *was* a novice," Haruki said darkly. "But, judging from what I heard last night, he most definitely isn't."

"The lady at the establishment Serena took me to said I was a fast learner," Nate murmured, flipping sausages.

Haruki spat out his coffee. Drake dropped his empty cup.

Callie's eyes rounded as the mug crashed noisily on the floor. "Wait, what?!"

All eyes locked on Serena.

"You took him to a—*a brothel?!*" Callie stammered, aghast.

"How uncouth," Sebastian murmured in a disgusted voice.

"You go, girl," Haruki mumbled, wiping his mouth and chin with a napkin.

Drake muttered something under his breath as he went to grab a dustpan and brush out from under the sink.

Serena sighed at their expressions. "It was the day before our first mission. Nate was wound up tighter than a spring. Lou and Tom threatened to put a bullet through his head if I didn't do something to get him to relax." She shrugged, not looking in the least bit guilty. "So, I got him to relax."

"A brothel," Callie repeated, pale-faced.

"The place was clean and I gave him protection," Serena added blithely.

Smokey hopped into the kitchen. He headed straight for the range and stared entranced at the tray of grilling bacon inside. A shiver raced across his fur. He looked over his shoulder. His rabbit eyes rounded when he spotted Sebastian.

"Good morning, brother," Sebastian said with a grave dip of his chin.

Smokey darted behind Callie and peered out at Sebastian between her ankles.

Artemus sauntered into the kitchen, mouth open on a yawn and fingers scratching his chest lazily. "Why is everybody up so early? It's Sunday." He stumbled to a stop when his gaze landed on Sebastian. A frown darkened his face. He looked accusingly at the others. "What is *he* doing here?"

"He's your new tenant," Serena said.

Artemus opened and closed his mouth soundlessly. "*What?!*"

Sebastian cleared his throat and removed a bundle of paper from his vest. "Speaking of which, I believe I have yet to sign a lease. I took the liberty of drawing one up. I hope you will find it to your satisfaction."

He pushed the contract toward Artemus.

Artemus swore and snatched it off the table. "Look, I don't know what you're up to, but no amount of—*holy shit, how many zeroes?!*"

He gaped at the sheet in his hand, reached blindly for a chair, and sat down heavily.

Serena peeked over his right shoulder. She scowled at the sum Sebastian had penned on the lease agreement. Drake whistled softly as he peered over his brother's left shoulder.

"I sure as hell hope you're not thinking of raising our rent," Serena told Artemus grimly. "Unlike Richie Rich, Yakuza boy, and the ditzy heiress over there, Nate, Drake, and I need to work for a living."

Artemus ignored her and started counting zeroes on his fingers. "I think I need to go lie down."

He rose and headed unsteadily out of the kitchen, the contract hanging limply from his fingers.

He came back a moment later, a puzzled look on his face. "Since when do we have an elevator?"

Serena frowned. "We have an elevator?"

"There's an elevator under the stairs. It wasn't there yesterday." Suspicion darkened his eyes. He turned stiffly to Sebastian. "In fact, it looks similar to the one that was in your home, in Salem."

The others stared at Sebastian.

"I made some renovations last night," Sebastian stated calmly. "We have a new basement."

Artemus's jaw dropped open. He stormed out of the kitchen.

"What did you do?" Callie said hoarsely.

Serena grinned. "I think I know the answer to that

one." Admiration brightened her face. "You moved your library here, didn't you?"

"All seven floors," Sebastian murmured. "And the boiler room."

"How?!" Haruki blurted out.

Serena rolled her eyes at him. "He used a rift, obviously."

"You are very perceptive," Sebastian said grudgingly.

"And you didn't tell Goldilocks?" Drake said, shocked.

Sebastian straightened his newspaper. "He will know soon enough."

"Dude, I'd start running if I were you," Haruki said with a glassy expression. "That guy's going to lose his shit. We're talking Doomsday level of wrath here."

Sebastian frowned. "What is he going to do, smack my bottom?"

Haruki paled. The others looked at him guiltily.

"We promised never to talk about the Qing Dynasty incident," the Yakuza heir mumbled.

Horror washed through Sebastian. "Wait. Are you saying Goldi—I mean, Artemus spanked you?! But you are the Colchian Dragon! A divine beast, no less!"

"That guy is insanely strong in his angel form."

Dread coiled through Sebastian for the first time that morning. "Well, I have yet to hear any protests coming from him."

They strained their ears, Smokey included. Bar the sound of cooking food, the house was quiet.

"Wait for it," Drake murmured.

A distant scream echoed from the depths of the mansion.

"*SEBASTIAN!*"

Serena pointed helpfully. "Back door's that way."

THE END

AFTERWORD

Thank you for reading AWAKENING! FORSAKEN, the next book in LEGION, will be coming soon.

If you enjoyed AWAKENING, please consider leaving a review on your favorite book site. Reviews help readers find books! Join my VIP Facebook Group for exclusive sneak peeks at my upcoming books and sign up to my newsletter for new release alerts, exclusive bonus content, and giveaways.

Have you read HUNTED, the first book in the SEVEN-TEEN series, the prequel to LEGION?

Turn the page to read an extract from HUNTED now!

HUNTED EXTRACT

PROLOGUE

My name is Lucas Soul.

Today, I died again.

This is my fifteenth death in the last four hundred and fifty years.

~

CHAPTER ONE

I woke up in a dark alley behind a building.

Autumn rain plummeted from an angry sky, washing the narrow, walled corridor I lay in with shades of gray. It dripped from the metal rungs of the fire escape above my head and slithered down dirty, barren walls, forming puddles under the garbage dumpsters by my feet. It gurgled in gutters and rushed in storm drains off the main avenue behind me.

It also cleansed away the blood beneath my body.

For once, I was grateful for the downpour; I did not want any evidence left of my recent demise.

I blinked at the drops that struck my face and slowly climbed to my feet. Unbidden, my fingers rose to trace the cut in my chest; the blade had missed the birthmark on my skin by less than an inch.

I turned and studied the tower behind me. I was not sure what I was expecting to see. A face peering over the edge of the glass and brick structure. An avenging figure drifting down in the rainfall, a bloodied sword in its hands and a crazy smile in its eyes. A flock of silent crows come to take my unearthly body to its final resting place.

Bar the heavenly deluge, the skyline was fortunately empty.

I pulled my cell phone out of my jeans and stared at it. It was smashed to pieces. I sighed. I could hardly blame the makers of the device. They had probably never tested it from the rooftop of a twelve-storey building. As for me, the bruises would start to fade by tomorrow.

It would take another day for the wound in my chest to heal completely.

I glanced at the sky again before walking out of the alley. An empty phone booth stood at the intersection to my right. I strolled toward it and closed the rickety door behind me. A shiver wracked my body while I dialed a number. Steam soon fogged up the glass wall before me.

There was a soft click after the fifth ring.

'Yo,' said a tired voice.

'Yo yourself,' I said.

A yawn traveled down the line. 'What's up?'

'I need a ride. And a new phone.'

There was a short silence. 'It's four o'clock in the morning.' The voice had gone blank.

'I know,' I said in the same tone.

The sigh at the other end was audible above the pounding of the rain on the metal roof of the booth. 'Where are you?'

'Corner of Cambridge and Staniford.'

Fifteen minutes later, a battered, tan Chevrolet Monte Carlo pulled up next to the phone box. The passenger door opened.

'Get in,' said the figure behind the wheel.

I crossed the sidewalk and climbed in the seat. Water dripped onto the leather cover and formed a puddle by my feet. There was a disgruntled mutter from my left. I looked at the man beside me.

Reid Hasley was my business partner and friend. Together, we co-owned the Hasley and Soul Agency. We were private investigators, of sorts. Reid certainly qualified as one, being a former Marine and cop. I, on the other hand, had been neither.

'You look like hell,' said Reid as he maneuvered the car into almost nonexistent traffic. He took something from his raincoat and tossed it across to me. It was a new cell.

I raised my eyebrows. 'That was fast.'

He grunted indistinct words and lit a cigarette. 'What happened?' An orange glow flared into life as he inhaled, casting shadows under his brow and across his nose.

I transferred the data card from the broken phone into the new one and frowned at the bands of smoke drifting toward me. 'That's going to kill you one day.'

'Just answer the question,' he retorted.

I looked away from his intense gaze and contemplated the dark tower at the end of the avenue. 'I met up with our new client.'

'And?' said Reid.

'He wasn't happy to see me.'

Something in my voice made him stiffen. 'How unhappy are we talking here?'

I sighed. 'Well, he stuck a sword through my heart and pushed me off the top of the Cramer building. I'd say he was pretty pissed.'

Silence followed my words. 'That's not good,' said Reid finally.

'No.'

'It means we're not gonna get the money,' he added.

'I'm fine by the way. Thanks for asking,' I said.

He shot a hard glance at me. 'We need the cash.'

Unpalatable as the statement was, it was also regrettably true. Small PI firms like ours had just about managed before the recession. Nowadays, people had more to worry about than what their cheating spouses were up to. Although embezzlement cases were up by a third, the victims of such scams were usually too hard up to afford the services of a good detective agency. As a result, the rent on our office space was overdue by a month.

Mrs. Trelawney, our landlady, was not pleased about this; at five-foot two and weighing just over two hundred pounds, the woman had the ability to make us quake in our boots. This had less to do with her size than the fact that she made the best angel cakes in the city. She gave them out to her tenants when they paid the rent on time. A month without angel cakes was making us twitchy.

'I think we might still get the cakes if you flash your eyes at her,' mused my partner.

I stared at him. 'Are you pimping me out?'

'No. You'd be a tough sell,' he retorted as the car splashed along the empty streets of the city. He glanced at me. 'This makes it what, your fourteenth death?'

'Fifteenth.'

His eyebrows rose. 'Huh. So, two more to go.'

I nodded mutely. In many ways, I was glad Hasley had entered my unnatural life, despite the fact that it happened in such a dramatic fashion. It was ten years ago this summer.

Hasley was a detective in the Boston PD Homicide Unit at the time. One hot Friday afternoon in August, he and his partner of three years found themselves on the trail of a murder suspect, a Latino man by the name of Burt Suarez. Suarez worked the toll bridge northeast of the city and had no priors. Described by his neighbors and friends as a gentle giant who cherished his wife, was kind to children and animals, and even attended Sunday service, the guy did not have so much as a speeding ticket to his name. That day, the giant snapped and went on a killing spree after walking in on his wife and his brother in the marital bed. He shot Hasley's partner, two uniformed cops, and the neighbor's dog, before fleeing toward the river.

Unfortunately, I got in his way.

In my defense, I had not been myself for most of that month, having recently lost someone who had been a friend for more than a hundred years. In short, I was drunk.

On that scorching summer's day, Burt Suarez achieved something no other human, or non-human for that matter, had managed before or since.

He shot me in the head.

Sadly, he did not get to savor this feat, as he died minutes after he fired a round through my skull. Hasley still swore to this day that Suarez's death had more to do with seeing me rise to my feet Lazarus-like again than the gunshot wound he himself inflicted on the man with his Glock 19.

That had been my fourteenth death. Shortly after witnessing my unholy resurrection, Hasley quit his job as a detective and became my business partner.

Over the decade that followed, we trailed unfaithful spouses, found missing persons, performed employee checks for high profile investment banks, took on surveillance work for attorneys and insurance companies, served process to disgruntled defendants, and even rescued the odd kidnapped pet. Hasley knew more about me than anyone else in the city.

He still carried the Glock.

'Why did he kill you?' said Reid presently. He braked at a set of red lights. 'Did you do something to piss him off?' There was a trace of suspicion in his tone. The lights turned green.

'Well, broadly speaking, he seemed opposed to my existence.' The rhythmic swishing of the windscreen wipers and the dull hiss of rubber rolling across wet asphalt were the only sounds that broke the ensuing lull. 'He called me an ancient abomination that should be sent straight to Hell and beyond.' I grimaced. 'Frankly, I thought that was a bit ironic coming from someone who's probably not that much older than me.'

Reid crushed the cigarette butt in the ashtray and narrowed his eyes. 'You mean, he's one of you?'

I hesitated before nodding once. 'Yes.'

Over the years, as I came to know and trust him, I told Reid a little bit about my origins.

I was born in Europe in the middle of the sixteenth century, when the Renaissance was at its peak. My father came from a line of beings known as the Crovirs, while my mother was a descendant of a group called the Bastians. They are the only races of immortals on Earth.

Throughout most of the history of man, the Crovirs and the Bastians have waged a bitter and brutal war against one another. Although enough blood has been shed over the millennia to fill a respectable portion of the Caspian Sea, this unholy battle between immortals has, for the most, remained a well-kept secret from the eyes of ordinary humans, despite the fact that they have been used as pawns in some of its most epic chapters.

The conflict suffered a severe and unprecedented setback in the fourteenth century, when the numbers of both races dwindled rapidly and dramatically; while the Black Death scourged Europe and Asia, killing millions of humans, the lesser-known Red Death shortened the lives of countless immortals. It was several decades before the full extent of the devastation was realized, for the plague had brought with it an unexpected and horrifying complication.

The greater part of those who survived became infertile.

This struck another blow to both sides and, henceforth, an uneasy truce was established. Although the odd incident still happened between embittered members of each race, the fragile peace has, surprisingly, lasted to this day. From that time on, the arrival of an immortal child into the world became an event that was celebrated at the highest levels of each society.

My birth was a notable exception. The union between a Crovir and a Bastian was considered an unforgivable sin and strictly forbidden by both races; ancient and immutable, it was a fact enshrined into the very doctrines and origins of our species. Any offspring of such a coupling was thus deemed an abomination unto all and sentenced to death from the very moment they were conceived. I was not the first half-breed, both races having secretly mated with each other in the past. However, the two immortal societies wanted me to be the last. Fearing for my existence, my parents fled and took me into hiding.

For a while, our life was good. We were far from rich and dwelled in a remote cabin deep in the forest, where we lived off the land, hunting, fishing, and even growing our own food. Twice a year, my father ventured down the mountain to the nearest village, where he traded fur for oil and other rare goods. We were happy and I never wanted for anything.

It was another decade before the Hunters finally tracked us down. That was when I learned one of the most important lessons about immortals.

We can only survive up to sixteen deaths.

Having perished seven times before, my father died after ten deaths at the hands of the Hunters. He fought until the very last breath left his body. I watched them kill my mother seventeen times.

I should have died that day. I did, in fact, suffer my very first death. Moments after the act, I awoke on the snow-covered ground, tears cooling on my face and my blood staining the whiteness around me. Fingers clenching convulsively around the wooden practice sword my father had given me, I waited helplessly for a blade to sink into my heart once more. Minutes passed before I realized I was alone in that crimson-colored clearing, high up in the Carpathian Mountains.

The crows came next, silent flocks that descended from the gray winter skies and covered the bloodied bodies next to me. When the birds left, the remains of my parents had disappeared as well. All that was left was ash.

It was much later that another immortal imparted to me the theory behind the seventeen deaths. Each one apparently took away a piece of our soul. Unlike our bodies, our souls could not regenerate after a death. Thus, Death as an ultimate end was unavoidable. And then the crows come for most of us.

No one was really clear as to where the birds took our earthly remains.

'What if you lived alone, on a desert island or something, and never met anyone? You could presumably never die,' Reid had argued with his customary logic when I told him this.

'True. However, death by boredom is greatly underestimated,' I replied. 'Besides, someone like you is bound to kill himself after a day without a smoke.'

'So the meeting was a trap?' said Reid.

His voice jolted me back to the present. The car had pulled up in front of my apartment block. The road ahead was deserted.

'Yes.' Rain drummed the roof of the Monte Carlo. The sound reminded me of the ricochets of machine guns. Unpleasant memories rose to the surface of my mind. I suppressed them firmly.

'Will he try to kill you again?' said Reid. I remained silent. He stared at me. 'What are you gonna do?'

I shifted on the leather seat and reached for the door handle. 'Well, seeing as you're likely to drag me back from Hell if I leave you high and dry, I should probably kill him first.'

I exited the car, crossed the sidewalk, and entered the lobby of the building. I turned to watch the taillights of

the Chevrolet disappear in the downpour before getting in
the lift. Under normal circumstances, I would have taken
the stairs to the tenth floor. Dying, I felt, was a justifiable
reason to take things easy for the rest of the night.

My apartment was blessedly cool and devoid of immortals hell-bent on carving another hole in my heart. I took a
shower, dressed the wound on my chest, and went to bed.

➤ GET HUNTED NOW!

BOOKS BY A.D. STARRLING

Hunted (A Seventeen Series Novel) Book One

'My name is Lucas Soul. Today, I died again. This is my fifteenth death in the last four hundred and fifty years. And I'm determined that it will be the last.'

Warrior (A Seventeen Series Novel) Book Two

The perfect Immortal warrior. A set of stolen, priceless artifacts. An ancient sect determined to bring about the downfall of human civilization.

Empire (A Seventeen Series Novel) Book Three

An Immortal healer. An ancient empire reborn. A chain of cataclysmic events that threatens to change the fate of the world.

Legacy (A Seventeen Series Novel) Book Four

The Hunter who should have been king. The Elemental who fears love. The Seer who is yet to embrace her powers. Three immortals whose fates are entwined with that of the oldest and most formidable enemy the world has ever faced.

Origins (A Seventeen Series Novel) Book Five

The gifts bestowed by One not of this world, to the Man who had lived longer than most. The Empire ruled by a King who would swallow the world in his madness. The Warrior who chose to rise against her own kind in order to defeat him. Discover the extraordinary beginnings of the Immortals and the unforgettable story of the Princess who would become a Legend.

Destiny (A Seventeen Series Novel) Book Six

An enemy they never anticipated. A brutal attack that tears them apart. A chain of immutable events that will forever alter the future. Discover the destiny that was always theirs to claim.

The Seventeen Collection 1: Books 1-3

Boxset featuring Hunted, Warrior, and Empire.

The Seventeen Collection 2: Books 4-6

Boxset featuring Legacy, Origins, and Destiny.

The Seventeen Complete Collection: Books 1-6

Boxset featuring Hunted, Warrior, Empire, Legacy, Origins, and Destiny.

First Death (A Seventeen Series Short Story) #1

Discover where it all started...

Dancing Blades (A Seventeen Series Short Story) #2

Join Lucas Soul on his quest to become a warrior.

The Meeting (A Seventeen Series Short Story) #3

Discover the origins of the incredible friendship between the protagonists of Hunted.

The Warrior Monk (A Seventeen Series Short Story) #4

Experience Warrior from the eyes of one of the most beloved characters in Seventeen.

The Hunger (A Seventeen Series Short Story) #5

Discover the origin of the love story behind Empire.

The Bank Job (A Seventeen Series Short Story) #6

Join two of the protagonists from Legacy on their very first adventure.

The Seventeen Series Short Story Collection 1 (#1-3)

Boxset featuring First Death, Dancing Blades, and The Meeting.

The Seventeen Series Short Story Collection 2 (#4-6)

Boxset featuring The Warrior Monk, The Hunger, and The Bank Job.

The Seventeen Series Ultimate Short Story Collection

Boxset featuring First Death, Dancing Blades, The Meeting, The Warrior Monk, The Hunger, and The Bank Job.

Blood and Bones (Legion Book One)

The Seventeen spin-off series is here!

I am darkness. I am light. I am wrath. I am salvation. I am rebirth. I am destruction. I belong to Heaven. I belong to Hell. P.S. I like bunnies.

Fire and Earth (Legion Book Two)

L.A. is teeming with demons. Only one man and his ragtag team of supernatural misfits can stop them.

Awakening (Legion Book Three)

Knowledge is power...

Forsaken (Legion Book Four)

They thought they knew who their enemy was...

Mission:Black (A Division Eight Thriller)

A broken agent. A once in a lifetime chance. A new mission that threatens to destroy her again.

Mission: Armor (A Division Eight Thriller)

A man tortured by his past. A woman determined to save him. A deadly assignment that threatens to rip them apart.

Mission:Anaconda (A Division Eight Thriller)

It should have been a simple mission. They should have been in and out in a day. Except it wasn't. And they didn't.

Void (A Sci-fi Horror Short Story)

2065. Humans start terraforming Mars.

2070. The Mars Baker2 outpost is established on the Acidalia Planitia.

2084. The first colonist goes missing.

The Other Side of the Wall (A Short Horror Story)

Have you ever seen flashes of darkness where there should only be light? Ever seen shadows skitter past out of the corner of your eyes and looked, only to find nothing there?

AUDIOBOOKS

Hunted (A Seventeen Series Novel) Book One

Warrior (A Seventeen Series Novel) Book Two

Empire (A Seventeen Seres Novel) Book Three

First Death (A Seventeen Series Short Story) #1

Dancing Blades (A Seventeen Series Short Story) #2

The Meeting (A Seventeen Series Short Story) #3

The Warrior Monk (A Seventeen Series Short Story) #4

ABOUT THE AUTHOR

AD Starrling's bestselling supernatural thriller series **Seventeen** combines action, suspense, and a heavy dose of fantasy to make each book an explosive, adrenaline-fueled ride, while **Legion**, the spin-off series, has been compared to Jim Butcher's **The Dresden Files**. If you prefer your action hot and your heroes sexy and strong-willed, then check out AD's military thriller series **Division Eight**.

When she's not busy writing, AD can be found eating Thai food, being tortured by her back therapists, drooling over gadgets, working part-time as a doctor on a Neonatal Intensive Care unit somewhere in the UK, reading manga, and watching action flicks and anime. She has occasionally been accused of committing art with a charcoal stick and some drawing paper.

Find out more about AD on her website www.adstarrling.com where you can sign up for her awesome newsletter, get exclusive freebies, and never miss her latest release. You'll also have a chance to see sneak previews of her work, participate in exclusive giveaways, and hear about special promotional offers first.

Here are some other places where you can connect with her:
Sign-up to AD's Newsletter
Follow AD on Bookbub
Follow AD on Amazon
Join AD's Facebook VIP Fan Group